A F*CKLOAD OF SHORTS

JEDIDIAH AYRES

All characters in this compilation are fictitious. Any resemblance to actual persons, living or dead, is purely coincidental.

A F*CKLOAD OF SHORTS

Copyright © 2012
Jedidiah Ayres

Published by Snubnose Press
Cover design by Eric Beetner

All rights reserved. No part of this book may be reproduced or transmitted in any form or by any means, electronic or mechanical, including photocopying, recording, or any information storage and retrieval system, without prior written permission of the Author. Your support of author's rights is appreciated.

TABLE OF CONTENTS

Introduction	4
Mahogany & Monogamy	7
Fuckload of Scotch Tape	35
Hoosier Daddy	71
The Whole Buffalo	96
Miriam	141
The Morning After	169
1998 Was a Bad Year	183
Amateurs	199
The Adversary	214
Viscosity	234
Nolte	248

Introduction
by Scott Phillips

People ask me to do things all the time. A wild-eyed former beauty, her matted hair dyed an unconvincing shade of black, approaches me on the street and asks "Mister, could you watch my monkey for a minute while I get my pap smear?" while the monkey, a tailless Old World species with a particularly angry snarl beneath his tatty fez, pulls at his chain in an attempt to bite my face. I tell her I'm no monkey's keeper and hurry away.

Or say a gruff stranger shows up at my front door holding an object wrapped in butcher's paper and asks if I'd be willing to cook him a couple of pork chops, explaining that he's a houseguest of one of my neighbors and has the use of their the kitchen but doesn't know how to cook. Do I cook it for him? Of course I fucking do not. I send him on his hungry way.

Or consider a scenario in which an old friend from school informs me he's started a new business, selling vintage clothing. He can't keep up with the demand for suits with wide lapels, poodle skirts and raccoon coats, and traditional sources for such items are stretched quite thin. I seem to remember you being good with a shovel, he says, and invites me to accompany him on a trip to our local bone orchard in search of fresh merchandise. Do I alert the authorities to his grisly plot? Of course not; I'm no monster. But neither do I assist him in the disinterment and denuding of our town elders!

And so you might imagine that when Jedidiah Ayres approached me with a request to write an introduction to the volume of stories you hold in your hands (more likely in one of your hands, given the prurient nature of the material herein) my reaction would be a violent "no!"

You would be wrong, however, because Mr.

JEDIDIAH AYRES

Ayres is my screenwriting partner, which is a way of saying that I conned him into helping me write some things, extracting from him several hundred hours of unpaid labor which he quite justly resents. I have been described as "conscienceless," a harsh judgment when you consider that it took only the threat of a lawsuit to get me to agree that perhaps I did owe him a little something in the way of an introduction.

The easiest way to start would be to categorize Jed's stories as mere delivery devices for a particularly warped kind of black humor and the kind of sex that might make Larry Flynt reconsider his position on the First Amendment. They're also insanely violent and if necrophilia is a deal-killer for you as regards fiction, look elsewhere. But if you're a degenerate and a pervert like me, you'll love every page of this sick little collection of the inner skull scrapings of a madman.

Mahogany & Monogamy

The first time I saw Janis I knew she was a ball buster. That was part of the appeal, honestly. Mom had been one and my kid sister, Denise? That's all I got to say. But Janis had something special and I'm not just talking about her industrial-strength rack and bear-trap thighs. She also had that elusive thing that I just can't resist, and if I knew what it was I probably wouldn't have a story to tell.

We had our own song, "Sweet Child O'Mine". It was our first dance. She danced, that's what she did, and when it got to the 'where do we go?' part, she slowed way down and tried to grind it outta me with her hips. Then she did something strange. She stopped and looked me right in the eye. It made me pop. She rocked my world with just a look, then kept on dancing. Sure, she helped lotsa guys do the same, but me? After the first time I saw her, there wasn't anybody else, you know?

You're never gonna find anything my old man said written down in a book. He was a loser till the day he died, fucked over and left by my mom, but he did manage one memorable line near the end when the lucid spells were brief and unpredictable. He was talking about when he first met my mother. He said he knew she was the one for him because she made him wanna grow up and produced the previously impossible in his life - mahogany and monogamy. I thought it was just a nice rhymey thing to say till that night.

Janis didn't notice anything special about me at first, and that was okay. Working at the Beaver Cleaver, she didn't meet many prizes, and to look at me, you'd not stop and think, 'guys a sex machine' or 'what's his secret?' But people change. They do grow up. They can surprise you sometimes. Gimme a chance and who knows? Could might be I make an impression.

MAHAGONY & MONOGAMY

Could be I'd made a life change. Could be I'd got my shit together. Could be I had fifty-thousand dollars in a gym bag in my trunk. Could be.

* * *

The thing about a guy like me having that kind of money on him? Yeah, it means somebody else is short that much. I never invested in stocks or had a business. I never went to high school or had anything fancy education-wise and I never paid taxes unless you count cigarettes. Which, come to think of it, maybe you should. Because, damn if they don't go up all the time, for real. So, yeah has to be somebody missing it.

The question then, is who?

Relax, might not be an Einstein or any other brainy heeb you care to name, but I'm not as dumb as you might initially think. It's not like I robbed a bank and got my picture took, or ripped off some solid citizen who'd wanna bring lawyers into a fair fight. And I aint about to take on no badass, because I know a thing or two about when I'm outta my depth.

No, it was just Benji, that skinny tweaker with the fuzzy upper lip you wanna scrape for him. Seriously, I'm no square, but damn, some motherfuckers just ain't intended to wear mustaches. I took it from a hole in the wall behind his medicine cabinet. Just stumbled onto it and took it.

Pee-Wee, the guy who runs Carl's Bad Tavern down off Cherokee? He sees me getting up to leave the other night and slips me twenty bucks to take Benji's ass home. Benji's passed out in the bathroom, puke everywhere except the fucking toilet and a cloud of that rat poison he smokes stinking up the place.

Not one to look a gift horse up the ass, I take the twenty and put him in my Chevette. Thought about just dumping him around the corner, because he stank like he'd been practicing, but I shut that shit down because it was time to get a little forward-thinking in my game. In the future, could be Pee-Wee knows I'm solid for this kinda thing. Could be he thinks of me first, next time. Could be some regular gigs coming, or at least a free drink now and then. Never know. Could be.

I wasn't about to fuck with that possibility by taking the man's money then not doing what it is he says he wants, like some short-sighted asshole who thinks he just played a man. So I took Benji back to his place, wasn't far, and let myself in with the keys I found in his pocket. Not a part I relished, reaching into a man's pants like that - especially a stank-ass motherfuck like Benji - but, like I said, I wanted to do this right. I was already thinking about future jobs.

Maybe I'd get some of those disposable rubber gloves, if this was gonna be regular. You know the kind they make them wear at Subway to make sandwiches? Or maybe, and this is even better, talk to my cousin Rob, the plumber. Find out what he does when he's gotta reach into some shit water and find a wedding ring, because you know plumbers don't fuck around when it comes to that. Hell, I could just get some Ziploc bags and put them on. Would be cheaper. If I paid taxes, I bet I could write that off.

I was getting a little carried away, but it felt good, being trusted with a job like that. Pee-Wee was a serious guy...shit... That was something else. Stop calling him Pee-Wee. He was connected to real people, and I didn't wanna blow any chance I had with him now by offending him. Herman hated that nickname.

The way I saw it, it was time to take a little responsibility. Time to think about a career. Not that shoveling shit outta bars was a career I'd like to have, but you know, it was a start. I'm sure Janis didn't wanna climb a brass pole for amateur gynecologists the rest of her life.

I brought Benji inside the door and no further. Fuck him if he thought I was gonna tuck him in or give him a bath. Not for twenty bucks. No way. But, I'd have a look around, thanks. It was how I made most of my money anyhow. A little B&E here and there, I wasn't above it. The beauty of this was, it was E without B, and Benji wasn't conscious the whole time, wouldn't have any idea how he got home when he woke up.

Benji was poor white trash, up and down. His basement apartment had plain white walls decorated with black light posters of like Pantera and hemp plants and shit. His clothes weren't in the dresser except for some underwear and socks, and those that were on the furniture and the floor were one pair of jeans - black and ripped, like the ones he was already wearing, and heavy metal t-shirts. There was no jewelry (surprise, surprise) and no electronics worth taking.

There were cassettes all over the floor, not in the

cases, which is something that personally really irritates me. It was the same story with the VCR stuff. Couple of tapes just marked with pen: Missing In Action, Running Man, Bloodsport. Say what you want about his lifestyle, his taste in movies was righteous.

Pisser was, I didn't find any drugs. Turned over his mattress, checked the freezer, behind the toilet, went through all his food, a jar of mayonaise, some Sanka and Kool- Aid. I was so frustrated, I went back to his grungy-ass bathroom and grabbed his razor. Didn't bother with any water or foam. Shaved that shit dry. Bled a little, but still looked better. Shit, that was two favors I did for him in one night.

When I put the razor back in the medicine cabinet, I noticed it was a little loose, like it was on a hinge or something. I gave it a little tug and it swung open, revealing a little hiding spot in the wall.

Fuck, there was a lot of money.

It was arranged in those neat little stacks you see rubber banded together in movies. I didn't even count it, just threw it in a gym bag and drove straight to the Beaver. I peeled off a couple hundred and went in looking for Janis.

Could've been my walk or the intensity in my eyes. Could've been the super- heavy testosterone vibes pouring off of me. Or could be she just saw me changing a couple c-notes for singles. Whatever it was, she knew right away that I was different. She put on "Sweet Child O'Mine" before I could even request it. She got every penny, too.

I started hanging out at Carl's every night. I'd keep my eyes peeled for losers ready to pass out or puke in the john. Fifty-thousand dollars was a nice start, but not exactly enough to retire on and I was serious about making a good impression on Herman. Besides, I couldn't tell anybody about my good fortune, because when a little shit like Benji had that kind of scratch? Right again, somebody else was missing it.

That was one thought causing me mild discomfort when it came up. How had Benji come upon that much money? When? And what the hell was he spending it on? I decided it wasn't my problem and I didn't want to know, so I shut down that negative shit quick. The way I saw it, if I kept up my regular schedule and didn't get flashy, I had it made.

MAHAGONY & MONOGAMY

The only change in my routine was stepped-up visits to Janis. Most nights, I'd come in with a single hundred-dollar bill and leave when it was gone. Though I realized I'd made a tactical mistake that first night bringing two hundred in and spending it so quickly. Janis had come to expect a little more from me, but so had I, and I was trying to show a little discipline. So it was one hundred every night...let's not go crazy, you know. I was trying to pace myself a bit and make her work a little harder for it.

Janis wasn't the only one working a little harder for her money either. Herman had noticed me and given me a couple more disposal jobs. Nobody I knew, though. I had to dig out their ID and find an address, and then I had to figure that shit out. Got to be, I was calling cabs and going with them to make sure they got inside. Oh well, it's like they say: you gotta spend money to make money. Yeah, I was, most of the time, blowing what Herman gave me on cab fare. But I was counting on that back end score once I got them home, and most of the time that worked out. A couple times there was a pissed-off wife or mean-ass dog waiting for me, but it was a safe bet anybody passing out at Carl's doesn't have much waiting for them at home.

***

I heard a preacher on the radio once say "Love is patient. Love is kind." All I could think was: he didn't love Janis. It was getting a touch restless between us. She was less patient, I was less kind, and we were becoming something of an item. One night during my dance I guess she felt I was being a little stingy because she stood up suddenly and said, "What the fuck Ethan? I am not doing one more number for a lousy hunnerd bucks. We're halfway through the first guitar solo and I barely got thirty-five outta your tight ass!"

Well that pissed me off a bit. The way I saw it, I'd been spending my money on her exclusively for some time now and hadn't got so much as a friendly hummer to show for fidelity.

"At least one of us still has one," I said, and left with money in my pocket for the first time. I decided she'd got her last score off of me.

Did I stop going? Hell, no. I still went every night after leaving Carl's, but I wasn't a one woman man anymore. No, I spread the wealth. New girl every night. I'd watch Janis out the corner of my eye and I could tell my being there pissed her off. The tension between us could tune a piano. Could be our thing had gone to the next level. Could be I was in my first serious relationship. Could be, I was finally growing up. Could be.

The night they broke Benji's arm, everybody assumed it was over sports action. It happened from time to time. That or drugs. Everybody knew that happened when you fucked around with the drugs. I had to keep it to myself that I suspected it had more to do with some missing cash.

He came into Carl's, his right arm hanging off him like a purse. He clutched it with his left, but was stumbling and running into shit every few steps. When he used his left to steady himself, the right would swing free and he'd scream loud enough to stop traffic in other neighborhoods. Before he passed out, he pleaded for somebody to get him a fix and get him fixed, just don't take him to no hospital, he had warrants.

He should've been a little more cautious about the company he'd make an announcement like that in, because there's a couple sick puppies in there just curious enough to try setting his arm without any idea of what they're doing. And nobody was gonna give him any drugs without cash up front.

When those dudes got tired of playing with his arm, I nodded at Herman, who took out a fifty this time. When I came to collect it, he grabbed me and whispered, "Take it easy tonight, huh?"

I looked into Herman's eyes and my asshole puckered. That guy looked scary. Maybe I'd just met the edge of where my hard ass turned to pussy, but he was like E.F. Hutton or some shit - I was listening.

"No hospital. Get him a fix." So, what do you think I did? I knew the arm needed to be set and secured, but shit, I mean, I didn't know any better than those biker fucks what I was doing. At least I scored him some good shit. Some shit anyhow. I never trucked with that stuff, so I don't really know from quality, but he slept through it all and I wandered alone in his apartment again. I think the place had been tossed, but it was hard to tell.

I felt a bit responsible looking at the kid, laying there with his busted wing, bound with a fuckload of scotch tape. I stopped for just a moment and let the feelings match up to thoughts about what exactly my role in this had been. It was a rare quiet moment of reflection for me.

"Look. You fucked up. That's who you are; the guy who fucks up. I'm just the guy who benefited this time. The way things go, man. No hard feelings."

He groaned through his opiate stupor and I continued.

"If it makes you feel better, I aint blowing it on pussy anymore. I mean, yeah a little bit, but I got bigger plans then that." In truth, I felt a little guilty. In fact, I didn't even get a dance that night.

I was back the next night, though. Lil' Debi was starting to get the bulk of my business. I'm not sure if it was her looks or style or what. She had big bangs that were stiff if you touched them and favored a very strong Strawberry scented perfume. It kinda smelled like she'd used a whole pack of chapstick on her crotch and maybe she had, but I suspect the real appeal was her name. There was something kinda kinky sexy about thinking I was getting dry humped outta my money by a snack cake.

Since Janis was there, I was playing my usual Motley Crue pick, "Don't Go Away Mad (Just Go Away)". I liked to think it bugged the shit outta her. I closed my eyes at the moment and sought out Janis's gaze with my mind. It pleased me to find it white hot at the base of my skull, and I savored it a moment, knowing that the jealousy of a woman tasted sweet.

So, it shocked me when I opened my eyes and saw Janis on the other side of the room, not paying me no nevermind. So surprised I was that I pushed Debi off my lap unceremoniously and spun around to see who it was looking at me.

Couple mopes dressed in nylon track suits and wearing jewelry, just bringing down the property value over in the corner, talking with Don the bartender. Following his pointing finger over in my direction. Didn't stick around to find any shit out, didn't help Debi up. Just left quick, before they could talk to me.

Five in the morning, my phone woke me up. "Mmmm..."

Whispered: "Ethan?"

"Mmmm."

"Hey, I just got off. I need to see you." "Janis?" "We need to talk. Meet me at Uncle Bill's." I found Janis at a booth, three Kools in the ash tray and one in her lips. She

shoved the coffee she'd ordered for me into my

hands. "Hope you like cream and sugar." She let me finish the coffee in silence, watching me intently while the whites of her eyes swelled with deep drags of menthol. She held my empty hand and sent electric tickles up and down my arm with her touch. The look in her eyes was intense and expectant - if our song was playing, I'd probably have wet my pants. It should have scared me, but I was only flattered. When I set the empty cup down she said, "So?"

"Yeah?"

"What did you do, Ethan?"

"What are you talking about?"

"Why are those scary guys looking for you?"

Immediately I half stood and looked around. "What guys?"

"You know, the ones at the club? What do they want from you?"

I shook my head. "I don't know. I've never seen them before."

She smiled and grabbed both my hands in hers. "You can tell me, baby."

Apparently it was some kind of turn-on. Danger hung off me like ten inches. We got a room at the Motor Inn and danger threw a party. Afterward, she slept and I watched TV till she got up about noon. Her makeup was a mess and her Tawny Kitaen hair bunched at odd angles from all the product and sweat and sleep. Her eyes worked hard at a twinkle when they met mine, but and maybe it was the daylight and not insincerity, the effect was sexy as...well not very. But when she dropped the sheet and walked to the bathroom, there was a pleasant tingle south of my navel.

I'm not sure what she'd heard from loose talk at the club or what she'd managed to get out of me during our little romp. Could be she's smart. Could be she's wired with a sixth sense for money matters. Could be I'm transparent. Could be... Because when she comes out of the shower a few minutes later, wrapped in a towel and looking sweet and fuckhungry simultaneously, she lets that little motel issue napkin fall and in the same instant nails me with, "So, how much we got?"

Nobody at the Beaver knew my last name. Janis had my phone number and that was it. She was the only one who could tell those scary guys in the sweat pants who I was. That made us partners, she figured. Partners in what?

Dude. Spending, of course.

Now, I'm not hypnotized over snatch so bad I can't see what's going on here. But come on... I am just exactly what you think I am: horny, lonely and a bit low on the old self-esteem. And if not this, then what the fuck is it money is supposed to buy for you?

So? "Fifty."

"Fifty!" she says like I just won her the teddy bear popping balloons at the fair.

"Fifty-thousand bucks, baby. All for us."

* * *

Being the meat in a fuck sandwich with Linda Carter and Erin Gray? Flying co-pilot with Jan-Michael Vincent? The Hair Club for Men? These were things I had given serious thought to over the years. Life expectancy was not. Had I devoted some time in consideration of it, could be some things I'd have done different.

Could be I'd not have started smoking at eight years old. Could be I'd never have told that loudmouth Brian Belisle about fingering Tanya Hopeck behind the dumpsters in Jr. High. Could be I'd not've stuck around St. Louis after stealing fifty-thousand dollars.

Might've turned out I'd not been such a sickly kid, gotten my ass kicked every day by Jeremy Hopeck or into some serious shit with an opportunistic stripper. But I'll tell you what, nothing would've stopped me from smoking, fingering or stealing in the first place.

It was going to take a couple days for Janis to wrap up her affairs. Minor things like getting some money she was owed and finding somebody to take her cat. But the plan was to leave town together, go to Vegas or New Orleans, live fast and loose for a while. Forget my future working for Pee-Wee. Guess I could call him that again...not to his face mind you, but he scared me too much to wanna be around. I was gonna see how much happiness, or at least pleasure I could make the money good for.

In the meantime, we agreed it would be best for us to continue our regular routines, so as not to call attention to ourselves. At least she should. I'd already got some attention. So, I gave her a thousand in walking around money. Enough, I figured, for her not to nag me for a bit, and too little for her to split on me with. She left me at the Motor Inn for work around six.

MAHAGONY & MONOGAMY

I was too antsy to stay at the motel, so I jumped in my car for a drive. Flipped the radio to 94.7 and scored an omen. "Sweet Child O'Mine" blasted from my shitty speakers and I rolled down the window, wishing my hair were still thick enough to wear long. It'd feel good to let it whip around in the breeze while driving. Crossed the Martin Luther King into Illinois and started cruising the east side, thinking long as she was playing this whole relationship mercenary style, might as well get some strange while the getting was good.

The song ended and another G'N'R tune immediately kicked in, must be two-fer Tuesday or some shit. "I used to love her, but I had to kill her..." I sang along, nodding my head at the simple sage-ness of the saying, "...and I can still hear her complain." Deciding to check out the Ten Foot Pole, I headed south. That's when the omen took a darker turn.

Normally, you can't catch shit on the radio. Seems I always have to twist the dial immediately after one good song, so back-to-back ass kicking tunes usually make my day - let alone Guns followed by AC/DC. But the thoughts I was beginning to have? Shit was dark. "Got You By the Balls" followed by "Dirty Deeds Done Dirt Cheap" sunk my mood. For real.

* * *

Would you be surprised to find out she'd told the six-million dollar man and his butt-buddy exactly who I was and where I lived? Okay, she didn't know, herself, but she knew my name and I'm in the book. So, no, I wasn't too surprised either, to come home to wash Ginger and Mary Ann off of me and find my apartment torn up.

I smiled a little smile, knowing that they hadn't found shit. I thought of zero sum nights, rooting around somebody's home, going through drawers and closets and under rugs, behind paintings and coming up empty handed. I thought of how frustrating that can be and the smile grew a little broader.

"Fuck you greasy fucks," rolled off my tongue as cool and understated as Bruce Willis might ever accomplish. I grabbed some clean clothes and skipped the shower. Who knew if they were watching the place? I went out the back door and down the fire escape. Even if they saw that much, I knew I could lose them down the alley and I'd parked the car three blocks away in caution.

I crossed the river again and ditched the car. I staked out the Beaver, waiting for Janis to get off. It was a long wait, but I didn't mind. I was savoring the thrill of playing the game a step ahead of these yo-yo's. Janis came out half-past four, with three other girls and a big ape. The girls got to their cars, the bouncer went back inside, and I did a half-crouched run up to Janis's passenger side.

"Judas Priest, Ethan! You scared me," she exclaimed as I let myself in.

"Hey baby, I just couldn't wait to see you." I kissed her and felt the hesitation on her end. Could be she thought she'd never see me again. Could be she was afraid I knew about her betrayal. Could be she was scared of what I might do. Could be.

She recovered quick, though. She smiled and grabbed my junk while she stuck her tongue down my throat. "You're supposed to lay low, but I'm glad you're here."

"Baby Doll, I hope you got paid, because I've decided. Fuck your cat, we're leaving tonight." See how she likes that.

She didn't. She looked concerned. Chewed on

her bottom lip for a second, but just like the calculating cunt I knew she was, she improvised just swell. Switched gears and went with plan B. "You're right. I don't wanna come back to this shithole ever again. Let's go now!" She kissed me quick and started the car, all smiles. The sincerity of the twinkle in her eye chilled me. Felt like a block of ice in my intestine.

I sat back, a little unnerved and said, "Airport."

* * *

At least, I'd taken the liberty of changing our plans. Miami never came up in our talks, so I figured I'd be safe enough there to do what I had to before disappearing for good. Now I needed to take the driver's seat, be the man here.

She played it through convincingly enough, if I hadn't known better. She even liked my new assertive style. It was different for her, following the leader. At the Beaver, or any other place like that, the women control everything and tell you how it is.

She slept against me in our first class seats and I pretended it was sweet. I pretended we had a future and were a team. I pretended all the way to the hotel, all the way through room service and the lazy sleepy sex before the nap.

MAHAGONY & MONOGAMY

I woke up an hour later and looked at her lying on her side, turned away from me. I let some light in through the window and took in the view. Really was something. I thought I should find another girl soon and come back here again. I turned around and looked at Janis. Looked clean and sweet and had that something - that definite something I still couldn't put my finger on. I slipped back into pretend mode, and while I was there, thought about our future.

Took a long hot shower. Scalding, really. Stood under the stream, walking through what I had to do. When I realized the hot water wasn't going to run out, I turned it off and scrubbed myself completely pink with those big white towels. When I stepped out of the bathroom, Janis was sitting, the sheet pulled up to her armpits, talking on the phone. She was whispering into it while I looked at her from the doorway.

Snapped me back. She never missed an opportunity. In truth, it made me love her just a little bit more. I thought: That's my girl. You're so smart. And capable. I want to be just like you someday.

She quickly hung up when she saw me watching. "Who'd you call?"

Beat. "Oh, just Trish at the club."

"Yeah?"

"Yeah, I told her I wasn't coming back to work and where the spare key for my place was. She's gonna take care of Angus for me."

"You tell her where we were?"

She looked at me, confused. "'Course not. I didn't say anything about a 'we'. Just said I wasn't coming back to work, would be gone awhile." She was pretty smooth, I gave her that.

I still had time for pretending, so I sauntered, yeah sauntered over to the bed and dropped the towel dramatically. She responded by rising to her knees and dropping the sheet. She smashed her world-class knockers against me and put her head on my shoulder. A regular Chrissie Hynde. I tilted her chin up to look at me and said, "Let's get married."

* * *

When I came back to St. Louis, six months later, I was tan. I was dressed smart, I even talked differently. I had come in to my own. I had gone into business for myself, used the money to buy in bulk. That's what they say: you gotta spend money to make money. And what do you know? They were right, this time. What ten thousand will buy wholesale will go for thirty, thirty-five retail.

And I wasn't out of my depth, like maybe you're thinking. Certain things you experience really prepare you for down the road events so that you know when the shit comes down, you're going to be ready. For me, it was killing Janis - when I drowned her that afternoon while she was talking about weddings and shit, like she was really into it. When we'd gone off to a private spot along the beach and she looked at me and said, "I want to spend the rest of my life with you," it was just the opening I was looking for.

I said, "Honey, you're going to," and did it right then and there. Knocked the wind out of her with a stomach punch, then onto her back in two feet of water while I sat on her shoulders. She died looking into my face, knowing I knew all about her plans for me, and I was reborn looking into hers knowing I was all grown-up now and could take care of myself.

We'd taken a trip out to Key West to celebrate our engagement and I left her without I.D. She'd had a few drinks by that time and had drowned, not been strangled, so I wasn't sure if they'd think she was a murder or an accident, but I didn't care much. I didn't think anybody'd try too hard to connect her to me, let alone find me across the country. I figured by the time anybody who gave a shit enough to put it together got around to my last known address, I'd have changed my identity and moved on.

And I did all that. I became John Connor, which was respectable enough. I figured the only thing looking for me was a cybernetic assassin from the future, and if he looked anything like Arnold, I could see that coming a mile away.

I came back to St. Louis for shits really. An odd feeling of destiny pulled me back just to look at the old stomping ground with my new eyes. I went to an afternoon ball game and drove through Soulard and Dutch Town just to see it again. I rolled up on Carl's Bad Tavern and thought, what the hell? and went in for a taste.

Nobody recognized me, which confirmed to me that I was one hundred percent changed. I casually sat at the bar and ordered a scotch, which I'd taken to recently. The bartender was new and I asked him where Pee-Wee was, used the name and everything.

He looked around nervously, hoping nobody'd

heard me and it tickled me to see the discomfort in his eyes. "Herman's out right now. You wanna leave a message?"

"Nah, just thought I'd say 'hey' if he were around." I finished my drink and got up to leave when one of the regulars - I couldn't remember his name - stopped me and said: "Hey, I know you, right?"

I looked him right in the eye and gently clapped his shoulder. "Not even close," I said, then took out a bill and put it on the bar in front of him. "Bartender, a drink for my new friend." And I was gone.

I spent the rest of the day sightseeing and stopped in for just a sec at the Beaver. What a shithole, I thought. Guess I'd come up in the world. Didn't even stay for a whole

minute. Went to PT's, which was more my speed now. Had a couple drinks and was getting a private dance when "Sweet Child O'Mine" came on the sound system.

Shit.

Wasn't prepared for it. Hadn't heard that song in months. Not ashamed to say, I got a little misty-eyed and sang along under my breath, "Now and then when I see her face...probably break down and cry." Nah, fuck that, I got up and left in a hurry. The girl called me an asshole and I didn't argue. I walked out and bumped into a couple unhappy patrons on the way to the door.

Was pacing, trying to wash the song out of my system, walking along the riverfront, on the way to the car. I always liked looking at downtown from the east side at night. The river rolling under the bridge was soothing with the lights from the casinos reflected on its surface.

"I used to love her, but I had to..," I whispered, to change the tune in my head.

Could be I was so intent on calming the fuck down, that I didn't see him follow me. Could be my thoughts were elsewhere all the way to the hotel. Could be he took me completely by surprise at the door, me thinking it was room service. Could be, but I'm not sure.

I'm not sure because I never saw his face, just the knife. Even when he stood over me after ransacking my room (rather poorly I'd say), I didn't have to look at his face to know who it was; just the way he stood there and the way his right arm hung funny.

So, I don't know. Maybe I was inviting it. Maybe I'd put it together some time ago. I mean, all the guy had to do was remember where he'd passed out. And maybe Herman told him who'd taken him home that night. Why not, right?

Fucking Benji, man.

Could be I wasn't so smart. Could be he wasn't so dumb. Could might even be she wasn't so guilty. Fuck. Could be.

Fuckload of Scotch Tape

It made Benji laugh any time he heard someone call them recreational drugs. He didn't know anything recreational about them. Maybe what he was doing, some would call killing himself, but he knew better. Killing himself is what he'd do if he wasn't doing what he was doing.

The kid had seen him. The way they'd worked it, he had to see somebody. Mr. Kent said they had to have contact and trust, and that meant Benji had to be seen. It was Benji because he was the low man. That's the way it always works. Shit rolls downhill and the grungy end of the plunger was his.

He hung around the mall for a couple days,

played some video games, and waited for the kid to be isolated. Then he had to get him in the van. Did they explicitly say grab him or threaten him? Did they say to tell the kid if he didn't man up and shut up he'd blind his sister and drown his dog? They didn't have to. They just said get him in the van and that implied do what you have to. That's what usually goes into convincing ten year old kids to jump into vans with strangers.

So he had. The kid went along quietly after the threats were leveled and sat there looking at him while Benji fumbled with the blindfold. Tears were falling freely, but the kid wasn't making a sound, he was too scared. Benji gave him the sleeve of his shirt to wipe his nose with before tying the bandana over his eyes. He told the kid to be cool and everything would be okay.

Liars go to hell.

Worse than actually grabbing the kid was keeping him. He couldn't see anything, blindfolded like he was, but Benji knew the kid remembered what he looked like and from now on when his image popped into the boy's mind, the rest of his life it'd be accompanied by hatred and fear like you reserved for the devil himself.

The fuck did he want a soul for anyhow?

* * *

Fifty thousand sounded like a hell of a lot more on the front end of the job. It was like four year's pay in a week and a half. He'd taken it on gladly. He'd been waiting for the opportunity to show Mr. Kent he was reliable and a stand up guy. They flew him to Dallas and he stayed in a hotel for free.

He didn't know anything about the kid or his family and that was for the best. Mr. Kent said that on this kind of thing, the more you knew, the more ways you could maybe fuck it up. Know nothing, you can't give anything away. That was another reason he got the job.

The kid's parents or grandparents or whoever the target was came through with the money and Benji never saw the kid again. Except in his dreams. Except in the mirror. Except every time he closed his eyes for a million years.

Fuck.

He'd seen it on TV completely by accident. The kid's picture flashed on screen saying he'd been kidnapped two weeks ago and that his body had just been discovered in the tall grass near the river. He thought he was going to puke. When the second picture, his own, flashed he stopped just thinking about it. Before he became one, the only patsy he ever knew of sang those sad ass echoey numbers that made him think of dad and gave him diarrhea. Guess he knew now, how come he'd got the sweet gig.

He hefted the money in a bag on his back and scrambled out the door. He jumped on a bus to anywhere and fucked the list in his mind. Dad, Kent, the money and himself in that order.

He took the bag off his shoulder and put it on the seat beside him, but the weight remained. That money would never spend. It was a part of him now, filling the place where his soul used to be.

He left Texas. Like that was hard. He cooled his heels in Bartlesville, Wichita and Jeff City before stopping in Dogtown. He found a basement apartment on the River Des Peres promenade and stayed inside it till the A.C. unit died for sure. He emerged pale and wasted and fat as a welfare check to watch the 4th of July parade, three weeks later. It was hot as fuck and sticky too. Your soul burns in hell, your body in the Midwest. It's not the heat, it's the humility.

He found work too, got a real job at the Courtesy Diner smashing beef patties to transparency from two to ten a.m. It was within walking distance, air conditioned and had a jukebox. He figured if he dropped his standards another couple notches he might even get laid.

Anonymous normalcy was the drug he craved more than any other. He came to an understanding that he was a world class shit, but found some facsimile of peace in it being a shit class world and told himself he didn't give a fuck. Still, he avoided reflective surfaces. And playgrounds. And malls.

Chuck, the other grill man, ex-marine, full time user and part time queer showed him around, and hooked him up. "Think you're some kind of hard case?" he asked, first time he saw Benj.

"Fuck's it to you?"

"Just that I'm the resident badass here, you've gotta settle for Beta-male."

"Whatever."

"You stay candy we wont have a problem." and he punched Benji's shoulder, good naturedly or neutrally, at least.

FUCKLOAD OF SCOTCH TAPE

"You the faggot, dude."

Chuck laughed. "Son, lemme clue you in, you're half a queer already and got some serious daddy issues to deal with. Could see that the moment you walked in. Give me a chance, I could be the mentor you so desperately need."

And he was.

First he taught him the double patty melt on white bread, then where to score. Benji lived on pharmaceutical adrenaline. It kept him up at work and most of the rest of the time too. It was important that he didn't dream or slow down. Muy importante.

* * *

Easing in to some downers, stretched out on his couch, Chuck said "Who're you kidding with that mustache, man? Have you seen a mirror?"

Benj stroked his fuzzy lip and smiled a natural smile for the first time in who the hell knows. "Fuck you, Grizzly Adams. Takes time to come correct."

"Look, keep it if you want, but you'll only get ugly chicks." Chuck dropped his voice an octave to show he was serious. "Time comes when you decide to walk on thewild side," he pulled out his USMC Zippo and flipped it a couple times before torching the cigarette dangling between his lips and winking. "Shave that shit, take my word."

It took Benji a moment to decide Chuck was fucking with him and then he laughed out loud. "Dude, will never happen. Poon hound. Snatch bandit. Hunnert percent."

They were watching movies with the sound down, or more accurately with the stereo drowning them out. Chuck was old school rock and psychedelia. Benji had metal and prog leanings. They compromised on Floyd and Rush and Zeppelin. "Here it comes, dude, turn down the music."

Chuck muted Warpigs and the chaos onscreen focused. He said, "See how big those guys are? No way. You ever seen pictures of real special ops guys? Normal to small size. All those muscles, that's pure Hollywood, bullshit."

"You're saying some puny guy my size gonna kick Action Jackson's ass, for real?"

"No, I'm saying Apollo Creed's never making rangers, is all. Let alone Terminator."

"I don't care, dude. This part's the shit."

"No doubt." Both stopped talking and watched the knife pin the Mexican or whatever to the post.

"Stick arowwn." They said in unison and high fived.

"The best!"

"Definitely."

Chuck was right. He had some serious daddy issues. Forget being good enough, he wasn't even there as far as his old man was concerned. His dad had drowned out the world with him in it from the time Benji was just five years old. Went to work, came home, fixed a drink and played records in his study with the door closed, till Benji's bedtime and there wasn't anything Benj could do to get his attention.

Dad was a suicide. He came home one night when Benji was twelve, fixed himself a drink, put on the Patsy Cline - or was it Ann Murray? - and blew his brains all over the family portrait behind the easy chair five minutes after Benjamin had gone to bed.

When Mr. Kent found him, he was living on the street, knocking over liquor stores and rolling queers to support himself and his growing narcotic dependency. Kent saw something he could use, in Benji and told him so. He promised Benji a place in the world and an education.

In the end, he'd delivered.

Benji's luck with father figures fucking sucked. Even Chuck betrayed him, eventually. Chuck said he couldn't be blamed for trying. Get past the patchy mustache, Benji was a good looking boy, and a brooder too. Chuck liked brooders.

What was it, he wondered aloud, one night, making that angel face scowl all the time? "You think I aint got baggage, kid? Hell, I was in South America most of the eighties. I worked with black marketeers trafficking organs and orphans to get to the drug cartels. Try remembering that every day. Or be like me and try forgetting. Point is I know you're carrying around some heavy shit, and as someone who's seen his share, I'm a safe place to unload."

So, he did. He came clean to Chuck about the kidnapping and the murder and changing his name. He told him about his nightmares and the drugs and how utterly alone he felt. He said he had no idea how the mustache looked. He hadn't seen a mirror in weeks because the kid was always there, waiting. Just sniffling and waiting. He told Chuck he had fifty thousand dollars in his apartment that he could never spend. Never because of what it had cost him. Every time he looked at it, he saw himself and everytime he saw himself, he saw the boy. Every time he saw the boy he thought he should kill himself.

And someday he would.

Chuck leaned in now, as Benj was in full blubber mode. He held his head to his chest and stroked his hair. He cradled him tight in his arms and shushed him like a baby. He stared into Benji's eyes with a look of solidarity. In that gaze he told him what he wanted to hear: That it was alright. He wasn't a monster. It wasn't too late. His soul could mend.

Then he slowly tilted Benji's chin up toward his mouth. He hesitated another second and then kissed him. It lasted maybe three seconds.

"What the fuck!" Benji snapped his head back and shoved him hard. "What the fuck, man?"

"Benji-"

"No. What the fuck did you just do, you fucking homo?" Benji got to his feet and began to pace in tight circles. "What the fuck what the fuck what the fuck." He'd be hyperventilating soon.

Chuck tried to calm him. "Kid- whoa, okay, bad move. Sorry." He reached out a steadying hand for him, but backpedaling Benji tripped.

"What the fuck what the fuck what the fuck?"

Benji pounded his fists on Chuck's apartment floor. He cried harder and thrashed about like a fish on land.

When he'd stopped his convulsions, Chuck helped him to his feet. "Look, let me get you a drink." He headed for the kitchen, but Benji grabbed his shoulder. Chuck turned around into Benji's best right cross. Hit him in the nose. Didn't break, but shit, it hurt. And the kid kept coming, cursing him the whole time. Eventually Chuck had to stop him with a gut jab.

But it was Chuck who sank to his knees while Benji collected himself enough to walk out.

Clutching his stomach with one hand and wiping his nose with the other, he managed, "Go to hell." going through the door.

Chuck nodded. "I'm sure we will."

Slam, crackle, pop. Benji coped.

* * *

He woke up hearing the kid in his head. "My dad is gonna kill me. Please please lemme go. You don't understand, he's gonna kill me. I wasn't supposed to be at the mall."

No shit. Fuck.

FUCKLOAD OF SCOTCH TAPE

He woke up and cursed himself for sleeping. Crack is wack, no doubt. It felt like somebody had fastened him to the floor with rubber straps. There was one around each leg, one on his waist and one over his neck. He lay there slowly registering where he was. Home. Living room. Floor. He had no recollection of the night before.

"If I don't take the dog out, my dad's gonna kill me. Please please please please please."

"SHUT THE FUCK UP!"

He wasn't sure if he'd actually yelled, but his head was clearing. "You can let me go. I won't be mad at you. I won't say a thing. I want to go home. Please please please."

Suddenly he was overcome with a suicidal notion. It got his blood up, got his body responding, and got him to the kitchen. There was nothing usable. Then he remembered a razor in the bathroom. Get there.

He did and was disappointed to see he still registered in the mirror. Vampires didn't have souls, and they didn't reflect either. What wouldn't he give to be one. The kid was there too, hovering over his left shoulder, just blubbering silently. Pitiful. "Shut the

> fuck up. I'm doing it already."

He grabbed his razor, but something stopped him. Something was wrong. Something unusual. He saw himself in the mirror. It had been a while, but he was different somehow, other than being pale to the point of blue. He was...bleeding. He touched his upper lip. It was irritated and a little scabbed, and the mustache was gone. What the...

Then the blood surged to his brain and his eyes focused on the medicine cabinet. It was unhinged and there was an empty cache behind where there should have been fifty thousand dollars.

Suicide could wait.

* * *

He went to The Lab, a gay club Chuck had taken him to, and loathe as he was to admit it, had a pretty good vibe. There were always heavy beats and flashing lights in the air and just like soldiers, those faggots knew their drugs. You couldn't not score, really.

'Course to most of them, it was recreational.

He sat at a table there with some of Chuck's friends. They hadn't seen old Chuck for a couple of days, but why doesn't Benji hang out? Chuck may come around. It was fucking disco inferno in there. He slapped hands and head bobbed all the way around the booth. He sat down and focused on the music. Pet Shop Boys gave way to that tune by the body builder with the pony tail, gonna make you sweat. Way ahead of you, thought Benji, his old prick tease instincts taking over. He took off his shirt. It was hot.

One of them looked like another ex-soldier, about fifty with tattoos up and down his arms and crammed into some black leather pants, middle that used to be all muscle, spilling over the waist and draped in a purple silk shirt. He got really friendly and loose with his stash. He took Benj out back to do some lines and get some fresh air, whatever else happened.

Except what happened was when Benji snapped his head up, feeling the burn in the back of his throat and closed his eyes, the fag planted a kiss on him. Without thinking about it, Benji bit off everything that got stuck in his mouth. The soldier made a gargling scream and clutched his mouth with both hands. Benji spit out bits of tongue and lips and cheek and inhaled briskly through his mouth. The hot, metallic taste of someone else's blood was even better than the cocaine burn.

He fell upon the older man with his skinny arms and legs pounding, not doing much damage, but the guy was in shock, curled up on the ground. Benji straddled him and beat him till he couldn't lift his hands. The whole time he was yelling. "You tell Chuck, I want my money! I want my money! I want my money! It's my money! Where's my money?" The man stared over his head, unconscious and defeated.

Benj went through his pockets. He found money and drugs. He took both.

It was Chuck he wanted, but there were plenty of other queers around and he wasn't feeling too particular for a while. He went back to his old ways. He knew how to find them, and let them come to him. He let them get him isolated, just like the kid was. He was so skinny and young and vulnerable, and just asking for it, really. He let them get a touch and get in close. Then he fucked their shit up. It didn't get old. It only got better and sharper as he recited the list. Fuck dad, fuck Kent, fuck the money, fuck Chuck. Fuck me. In that order.

One night he went back to The Lab. It was stupid to the point of suicidal, but nobody ever accused Benji Metcalf of being a brainiac.

They were waiting for him. Six of them took him into the bathroom and one held the door shut while the others worked him over. He'd heard once that it didn't hurt so bad if you don't fight it. He fought anyway. Fought for everything he hadn't before. The kid hadn't. Just went right along. He had whimpered and cried some like a pussy, but never even tried to defend himself. This was a source of bottomless rage Benji tapped into. Fought for all he was worth, which wasn't much after all.

Finished, they supported him between them and hauled him out the back door, not an uncommon sight at The Lab. They dumped him in an alley several blocks away and he would have gone into shock, but when he hit the ground, a bolt of sheer agony opened his eyes. They sprang like a popped lock. The pain made his body work, though he could barely walk. His right arm was definitely broken and he operated like a zombie.

Made his way by instinct or blind luck into the

nearest bar he knew and opened his mouth. He went down screaming, begging for someone to help him, but not to take him to a hospital because he had warrants.

* * *

He woke up back home. Home and on his couch. Took a long time to focus. He was coming off heroin. What the fuck? He didn't remember taking any. It looked like the place has been tossed, but it was hard to tell. He couldn't move his arm. It was broken right, but also fixed. Sorta. He looked down and saw that it'd been fastened tightly to his torso in a make shift cast of tape. He'd never seen so much Scotch Tape in all his life. It circled his arm, which was bent sharply like a chicken wing, then it wrapped around his body countless times as if to keep him from flying away. He knew he didn't have any tape in the house either which meant that somebody had brought his ass home, shot him up, tossed his pad and stopped at the Wal-Greens for tape?

Whatever.

He retraced what he could from the night before. Faggots, broken arm, bar, oblivion. Fuck if you think he was going back to The Lab. He started at the bar,

FUCKLOAD OF SCOTCH TAPE

Carl's Bad Tavern, a rough neck spot in south city. It was a long and painful walk, but he felt alert when he arrived.

The daytime crowd was sparse and the bartender watched him struggle on to the stool with his gimp arm, bound in tape, exposed because he'd been unable to get the t-shirt over it.

"Benji Metcalf, what the fuck?"

"Where's Herman?"

"Got the night shift, you know that."

"Could you call him?"

"Fuck no. He's sleeping now, or playing with his kid. I'm not gonna interrupt either of those for anything you've got to say."

"Thanks."

"But I'll spot you a round on account of I heard about the other night."

"Yeah, what'd you hear?"

"Heard your shit was fucked up. Heard you passed out, and somebody had to take you home. You can't be making a habit out of that, by the way."

"Sorry."

"It's not the first time, is all I'm saying."

It's not? thought Benji.

"Anyway, the drink is for your friend. I heard about Chuck." The bartender raised his own glass and clinked it with Benji's, resting on the bar.

Gravity tugged just a little harder at Benj. He felt he might slip off the stool. "What did you hear?"

"Died. Found him yesterday. Of an overdose."

"What?" He felt sat upon. It hit him harder than he'd have guessed it could have. He hated Chuck, right? Fucking homo made a move on him and stole his money, right? Didn't matter. Chuck was all he had.

"Accidental, I heard. Didn't you know? Sorry, dude. I got your next round too." Benji knew better than that. It wasn't an accident any way you sliced it. Those soldiers knew their drugs. Question begged then, suicide or other?

"Know who took me home?"

"Nope. You'll have to come back later. Talk to Herman."

He opted to sit in a corner booth the rest of the afternoon, and thought about Chuck. Thinking never cleared issues in Benji's experience, only clouded them. He was miserably confused. Maybe, if he was dead, he could be removed from the fuck list. Benji'd never really wanted him on it in the first place. He chewed a couple of pills and the adrenaline lift said that Chuck wasn't worth stressing out over. Fuck it.

Herman came in around eight and told him some that some guy who runs a few errands for him, took him home.

"What's his name?"

"Ethan, I think."

"Know where I could find him?"

"Try the East Side."

* * *

The East Side. Across the river, it was stripperville. He thought beaver should be the Illinois state animal. Where to check? He got a description of Ethan from Herman's bar back, but it was pretty vague. Still, a lead was a lead. He crossed the Eads Bridge, like it led to another country.

He started at the high end with the buffets, the ESPN and their hygienically and surgically superior women, but his instinct soon led him elsewhere. By the time he'd worked his way down the class ladder to the Beaver Cleaver, it felt right. That Slaughter anthem all the radio people seemed to think was the shit the year before was blasting from a $20 boom box on the three-foot stage. There wasn't any sawdust on the floor, but there should have been.

Three taut skinned, red boned youth sat at the front table watching one dancer, already disrobed and pointing her ass at them, doing a terrifically lude if uninspired and lazy number when he walked in. On closer inspection, he saw she was not dancing at all, but bent over at the waist, butt in the air, tits touching her knees, windexing the mirrored wall in back of the stage. She was vigorously applying the cleaner with a wad of newspaper where, in the course of her recent performance, she'd left cheek prints on the glass. A+, he thought. With the newspaper, it wouldn't streak.

Before she'd even finished, the next beauty queen came out sporting the rheumy, empty eyed gaze of a fellow traveler, and stopped the Slaughter tape, popping her own cassette in the boom box. Fucking hell. Richard Marx. Won't give up until we're satisfied. The bartender picked up a mic and let everyone know that it was Lil' Debi on stage, giving her all. He looked at her. She was shedding her outfit too quickly, stiffly and with all the grace of C3P0 on crank. She was demonstrating why pussy is like the sun - you never want to look directly into it - when the tape suddenly changed speed and then stopped altogether, leaving her splayed bare assed to the world without any musical accompaniment. Somehow it was too sad to look at.

In the void left by Dick Marx, Benji heard something that caused him to spin around in his seat so fast, he nearly fell out. In the brief moment before the dancer, unraveled her self from the pole, walked over to the boom box and switched to a radio station playing Firehouse, he heard the sound again.

It was remarkably like his own name.

Across the room, two heavies out of central casting were talking to the bartender and one of the other dancers. Benji slipped to the back of the room to watch. The foursome broke up a moment later and the two dressed like joggers left. He waited for the dancer to go back to work and hit her up for a private number.

It took a couple dances and a lot of cash to get the information out of her. The whole time she was bumping cluelessly into his busted arm. It shot regret all through his shoulder and into his head, but the story she told was fascinating.

He heard about some deal that went down in Texas a couple years ago. Some money had disappeared, fifty thousand dollars, and the bills were marked. There'd not been a trace of them all this time, until a few weeks back? It started showing up in the system.

"And guess what?"

She stopped bobbing on top of him for one second and he dared to ask "What?"

"It was spent right here at the Cleaver."

"No shit." He manages with a grimace as she punctuated her story by grinding against him again.

She got back up to full speed and Benji wondered what the chances were he'd get the Windex treatment afterward. "Anyway, they said they were Treasury Agents, but my boss has got his suspicions about that." she nodded toward the bartender, who was thumbing through the cash register, inspecting bills.

"So, who're they looking for?"

He nearly bit through his lip when she slapped his shoulder in excitement. "That's the best part! They wanted some guy named Metcalf, but I thought they should try out this creep called Ethan, comes in a lot.

FUCKLOAD OF SCOTCH TAPE

Said the money was hunnert dollar bills and he always had them. He has a thing for Janis." Without stopping she nodded her head in the direction of another girl at the bar, listening, wide eyed, to the bartender, probably getting the same story.

What she lacked in self awareness, she made up for with inhibition. She was such a committed pro, she tried to make her nodding head a part of the dance.

Back at Carl's Bad Tavern, Benji tipped the bar back heftily to match a last name to a first, and came away with Ethan Dillon. He got an address out of the phone book and found the place.

When he got there the sun was up. So was Ethan. He wasn't at home anyway. Benji let himself in and began to turn it inside out, looking for the cash. After a couple of hours the dregs of his last speed hit turn to sick in the hollow of his gut. Afraid of collapsing right there, he stumbled home.

* * *

When he woke it was dark outside again and it was dark in Ethan's apartment. Shit. He wondered if he'd slept through his opportunity to surprise him. If Ethan had come home and found the mess in his place, he might never come back. He sat in the booth at the diner across the street from Ethan's for an eternity, shoveling coffee on top of nothing. The tacky quality of his mouth encouraged him toward water, but he didn't pay it any attention. His kidneys felt like rocks.

The third time in an hour he noticed someone lighting a cigarette in the car parked outside, it dawned on him, the Treasury joggers must have found Ethan's place too. The focus of his stake out switched.

To say his arm itched underneath the tape would undersell it. It was, he felt, just going to be another loss in the continuing struggle for his sanity. He picked and tore at the edges a bit with the gnawed off fingernails of his left hand, but all that did was make it more raggedy than it already was. At first his arm had been securely fastened in there, but as he'd begun to sweat it had shifted around a bit. It gave off an alarming pulse of pain every time it moved, but he couldn't afford to sacrifice any alertness to pain killers.

He decided to go in for a closer look and ambled down the street with a cigarette in his left hand. As he approached the car with the windows down, he tried to look pitiful. It was not hard. He indicated his handicap as he opened a dialogue.

"Got a light?"

He named them in his mind. The Ranger looked out the window, bored. He was wearing a Mavericks tee shirt and a gold chain around his neck. "Fuck off" he said with a hint of the southern hostility in there.

"C'mon, dude, I'm not left handed."

Tonto leaned out the window with a lighter. He flicked it open and produced a flame. There was something familiar about it. When he snapped it shut, Benji caught the initials USMC across the top. The cocksucker had the same lighter as Chuck.

Oh shit.

* * *

Against his will, Benji started to think. There was a time and a place for it and he'd known neither. This sort of thing, the more you knew, the more you could maybe fuck it up. He had to keep it simple. Get this Ethan. Get his money back and forget revenging. Chuck was not worth it. The piece of shit had betrayed him, right? But he kept thinking.

The bills were marked. That figured. It meant

Mr. Kent had fucked him before he hired him. The Ranger and Tonto must work for him. No way they were Treasury, but they must've had some ties. Kent must have some connection with the feds who would let him know when those bills hit the banks. But how had they known his name? He'd not settled on Metcalf till he arrived in Dogtown, a year and a half after Dallas.

Chuck.

It was the only way that made any sense. It had to be. He hoped Chuck hadn't put up a fight. He had to stop thinking.

A light came on in Ethan's apartment. He watched them get out of their car and head in to the building. He waited a few before following.

Halfway up the stairs, he heard cursing. Ethan's door was open and the light spilled out with the sound of frustrated Texans. Ethan must've given them the slip when he saw the state of the place. The Ranger was out the back and halfway down the fire escape when Benji got to the door. Tonto was having a look see.

Before he could make a plan, Tonto was headed back to the front door. Benji ducked behind a wall, and waited for him to place himself near the stairs before hitting him. One armed, he had to take any advantage he could, but he felt a little sick and guilty when Tonto went over the railing and not just down the short flight. He heard the sound of bone negotiating with marble and the subsequent bounce to another short flight of stairs, three stories down.

He came around the first bend and saw the spot where the original smack had come from. It was slick and unlike anything you'd want to touch. Tonto had left a souvenir. Benji walked around it and resisted the impulse to reach out and let the bits of hair tickle his fingers.

There was a faint struggling sound, a sort of shuffling noise coming from the next landing and rather than look over the rail, he decided to descend the stairs one at a tie to give himself another moment to brace for it.

Tonto was in shock. He was lying on his back with his right arm and left leg pinned underneath him. If you didn't know better, you'd think he only had the one arm. Benji could see the spot, high on his forehead where the scalp had been torn away just a bit. It was too dark to know for sure, but Benji guessed, if he cleaned all the blood out of it, he'd be looking at bone. He leaned over the rail and wretched a thin line of mucous into the void. Tonto was looking directly at him, but not really seeing. The shuffling sound - he was trying to stand up. His right foot, like a bald tire spinning on wet concrete, was not finding purchase. It was on automatic, sliding uselessly over the dirty tile floor, again and again.

A black pool was behind his head, which brought out the white in his eyes. Benji got close enough to whisper to him. "You kill Chuck?"

Tonto's lips moved, but there was no sound. His pupils were expanding rapidly. Benj tried again. "You killed Chuck, right? You overdosed him, you and your friend?" Tonto stared straight ahead, his lips moving, but not saying anything. "You made him give me up and then you killed him, you son of a bitch. Fuck you."

He knew he wouldn't get an answer. Instead of waiting, he went through his clothes and relieved him of his car keys. He put his left index finger on Tonto's chin. He pushed down, making his mouth hang open and appear he was trying to raise his head. Benji leaned in and whispered. "I hope you hang in there a long time, asshole. Soak up all the pain, you got comin."

Out on the street, he teared up immediately. He had to swipe ineffectively at his watering eyes and running nose with the sleeve of his shirt. He hadn't really meant it. Benji hoped he was dead already. His vengeful notions had disintegrated as soon as the poor bastard went over the rail, but he had felt an obligation to see it through. Finish it the way it'd started.

The faces of his victims from the kid in Texas to the fags he'd rolled in parks and alleyways, they started appearing to him transposed onto Tonto's body, lying in an unnatural way on top of himself. They stared at him as if at the end of a long tunnel. He was glad they couldn't see him crying now.

It was a trick starting the car with his left hand, but thankfully the transmission was automatic.

* * *

His arm healed wrong. When he finally got the tape off after giving it a couple weeks, it hung at a funny angle. At the elbow it bent and dangled palm out. Looked like he was always about to shake your hand or thumb a ride. That's what Trish said, anyhow.

She was a dancer he'd come to know a little bit. In the past several months, he'd more or less given up finding Ethan and the money, but kept going through the motions of staking out Carl's and the Cleaver. He'd stayed straight most of the time too. He found out that Ethan's favorite girl, Janis hadn't been seen since Ethan had disappeared. Recovering that cash was not a realistic goal, but nobody ever accused Benji Metcalf of being grounded that way.

He kept the mustache shaved. Chuck was right, he looked better that way and he confirmed his sexuality every chance he got with Trish, which was more often than you might've guessed. He went to the Courtesy and got his job back, and got a new apartment that had hard wood floors. Looked good that way and trapped less dirt, he thought.

Took nothing with him. Not even a bed. He had a blanket he slept on top of in the warm weather and underneath when it was cold. Mornings the sun would pour in through his curtain less windows and he'd toss the blanket in the closet, then sit there in his clean, empty space and try hard at enjoying the nothing.

FUCKLOAD OF SCOTCH TAPE

He'd been sitting just like that one morning when there was a knock at his door. Nobody ever came over except Trish once. She'd laughed when she'd seen the place empty, and said they should go back to her's after all. Sure enough it was Trish, looking rougher than usual after a night's work. Her face is puffy and red more from crying, he thought, than blow.

When he opened the door for her, she hugged him and said "If you'd get a phone I wouldn't have to come over like this." He took her in and set her down at a sun spot on the floor. He rinsed out his cup in the sink and brought her some English tea he'd already brewed. It was part of the new him, not as reliable as a fix, but becoming just about as ritualistic.

He didn't ask her what was wrong. Figured she'd say when she was ready, or maybe never which would be fine by him too. But she didn't wait that long, said "Janis is dead." then started to cry again, her nose leaking onto her shirt. "Police came by the club last night. Said they'd identified her body. She died a while back. Drowned. In Florida. Said it looked suspicious."

She looked up at him. "Did you hear me? My

friend Janis is dead." He felt he should show some sign of remorse, but just couldn't fake it. "You know what? I bet it was that Ethan creep who killed her." It had poured out without consideration first. Just a gut reaction, he could tell. She sat there thinking it through and a few moments later, looked back up, but not at him. Certainty in her voice this time. "It was. I'm sure of it."

He tried not to think about it. Fuck. It was hard not to. His experience was, the more he knew... He was bound to fuck up. He felt something in the pit of his stomach at work that night and tried to imagine it was his recovering soul experiencing growing pains, but that didn't stick. This was darker. Uglier. Shit, it was vengeance again.

He was able to hold those feelings at bay by telling a few regulars at Carl's and the Cleaver to keep their eyes open for this Ethan guy. He gave them as good a description as he could and a beeper number and took to carrying it with him, though he intended never to use it. Its silence in his pocket was a lullaby that he went to sleep to every night. He took that much action and then stayed the hell away. He kept his head down, and told himself he'd done all he was going to. Then one day, it chirped.

It was a long hard walk up the street to the pay phone and he wasn't sure he would use it until it was already ringing.

"Hello, Benji?"

"Yeah?"

"Saw somebody, might be your guy at Carl's, just now."

"Yeah?"

"Yeah, except, he was dressed real nice, with a haircut and all. Had money,

bought drinks, too."

"He still there?"

"No. Just bought the drinks and left."

"Say anything?"

"Nope."

"Thanks."

It was nothing. Less than nothing. Didn't sound like the guy at all. Ethan Dillon was a low rent motherfucker, just like himself. He knew that much.

He was getting ready for work. He'd drawn the day shift some time back and was enjoying the hours. He knew he'd come a long way from the edge of suicide and insanity, and he knew it was suicide and insanity to go any further with revenge, but he told himself that was not what he was doing as he let the bus pass his stop at Hampton, where his job waited for him, and kept heading east. Toward the river. Toward the abyss.

* * *

Trish was off that night. Thank god. He wouldn't be able to control her, if she knew what he was doing there. She'd blow it, most likely. He sat at the bar with his back to the stage, watching the door, sipping Cokes and trying to shut out the shitty tunes for a couple hours before a Queensryche riff woke him up. He picked up his head just in time to see a well dressed version of Ethan Dillon turn on his heels, just inside the door and leave again.

Benji followed him outside. Well dressed Ethan walked a few blocks up to a higher class of shit hole and went inside. Benji entered and located him immediately. He had gone to the bar for change. He got a couple of drinks and then took up a solicitation for a private dance. Benji found a sentry position near the front door and waited.

Didn't take long. Cleaned up Ethan looked a bit shaken walking briskly out of the back and through the front door not two minutes later. Benji followed him humming Sweet Child O'Mine to himself into the night.

Ethan strolled along the river front looking like he might throw up for the first couple hundred yards, but eventually he recovered and found a taxi. Following suit, Benji trailed him west back down town all the way to his hotel and gave him a few minutes in

his room before he knocked.

The few minutes were really for him. He found the stairwell because he was going to need a couple lines to do it right. When he was ready he kept the knife in his left hand and knocked with his funny right.

Ethan Dillon didn't even see his face. Benji slashed him right through the neck near his shoulder. He stumbled a few steps and fell onto his back, a rich red fountain bubbling out of him. Benji shut the door and went through the room. He didn't really think he'd find anything, but while he was there...

There was no money, or I.D. or satisfaction. He came back to watch Ethan expire. He stood above, staring down, getting used to the view. That look on his face was familiar now. He'd seen it before and resigned himself to seeing it again in all likelihood.

There was a lurching sensation for a brief moment, when he cut the tether to his hopes and dreams of normality, but as any sailor would, he bore down, lowering his center of gravity and rode the wave. It felt like he was drifting slowly out to sea, away from his final port. He could still see land. He could still see solid ground and remember the sensation of standing and walking around on it, but he was never going back. It felt like he was looking into the horizon and seeing only a vast ocean, the void of space or a great black hole and he could only keep going. On and on. He didn't even have to take steps. He was drifting.

It felt like nothing.

Hoosier Daddy

Ty Crenshaw died. Sixty-two years old and fat as a cow, he'd suffered a fatal coronary climbing his own staircase after a midnight snack. The TV played old footage, non-stop, of skinny Ty with the duck's ass hairdo and cowboy boots and those sunglasses he'd only let slip to the edge of his nose for a split second to wet panties with his baby blues. They showed him playing his Rickenbacker like his nads were hooked up to the battery of his trademark beat up Chevy pickup. Then they showed clips from a handful of movies he'd appeared in like Mark of Cain where he'd played a reformed convict hitchhiking to Nashville to make his mark on guitar town and

Redneck Blues about a city girl whose car breaks down in nowheresville and then falls for her mechanic, a white guy who plays guitar in colored clubs by night. The coverage was endless and I found out all kinds of things about the hillbilly rocker I'd never heard before, about his copious cocaine use, numerous betrayals by managers and record companies as well as five adultery-ridden marriages, but what surprised me the most was that after all of it, how much money he was still worth. All that music and those cheap movies had made him wealthy and none of his bad habits had broke the bank. Good on him.

The news hit me harder than I'd thought it might. I guess growing up with his music always in the background had made it sink in deep. His were the records, playing in the house, that I'd drown out my own dad's cursing and threatening with. Mom would put 'em on when she felt a storm brewing and I'd play Star War or whatever with Ty's screaming electric twang soundtrack.

Mom finally left dad and took me with her, but

we left those records behind. Left everything behind, as it was one of that middle of the night escape jobs. I missed some of my toys and clothes and I missed my dog, but it never occurred to me to miss ol' Ty's music. So after he died, I became one of those late to the party enthusiasts of his. Hey, I'll own it; I've never been a big music fan. I couldn't tell you the names of the guys in Led Zeppelin and I don't know which of the Beatles is still alive or who exactly Nick Jagger was. All I can say is, when I saw the footage of that cracker on TV with the tight jeans and sunglasses, making sex to that guitar, so full of fight and life, and then pictured that he was dead? Maybe I cried a little.

Turns out, there was a lot of copiers, or people what they call "influenced" by Ty, still making music and they came through town playing concerts more often than you'd think. I started catching shows at Mississippi Nights and The Galaxy and The Hi-Pointe or The Way Out Club down on Cherokee a couple nights a week. I never bought the t-shirts or did the dances, but I'd stand near the front, watching and really listening to the music for the first time in my life.

It was powerful. It did things to me. Sorta molested me without me having any kind of say so. I won't say it was all pleasant. I'm not the type to let that happen. Don't like to be blindsided or surprised. I don't even go to movies anymore, ever since I saw Hoosiers back in high school. For some reason, I thought maybe it was gonna be a funny one, but it wasn't. And when Lex Luthor let that old rummy coach the game, I balled so loud that everybody turned around to look at me. When I noticed that they were staring, I went berserk, started screaming at all of them plus my own daddy, who was a rummy too. I threw my spit cup at the screen and it splatted and dripped down all over. Then I grabbed one of the guys looking at me and just about beat the piss right out of him.

So I'm not the touchy feeling type usually, and I've still got a temper on me, but that music was changing me, opening up new parts of me that I hadn't known were still around or even there to begin with. Sometimes in the middle of a song, I'd have to go lock myself in the crapper and have a little cry, but I wouldn't leave the show.

One night I was down on the Landing to catch

Junior Brown and got told at the door that the show'd been cancelled on account of sickness. That was a big disappointment. I was finding my tastes were drifting toward country music and Junior played it straight, but still batter dipped the shit outta his guitar sounds and had that deep authoritative quality to his voice that I really responded to. I didn't mind so much being made to cry by somebody that sounded like that, but I figured if one of those slick little shits from the radio ever turned me out I might as well put on a dress and suck on cock.

Since I was already down there in that nightlife area of town, by the river, I figured I might as well look around at the other attractions. Most places were featuring music that didn't do anything for me and they were attracting a young crowd - just dripping with entitlement and inheritance. But finally I found a place having a good old-fashioned titty show.

On stage there was a pale, skinny little girl with short hair of an unnatural color wiggling her ass not unlike those old movies of Ty Crenshaw, and unlike the slower more seductive movements of the tanned girls with bright teeth. I mean she was electric-fied; got-chiggers- all-over-me shaking, just mesmerizing me. Her name was Lila and all I could think to call what she had was spunk. She was one of the finalists of the wet T-shirt contest and clearly out of her league glandularly speaking. Still, she made a barn burner of it; giving the blond with the tits like furniture you could kick your feet up on, a run for the money. She smiled big and when the winner sought to extend the good sportsmanship gesture, Lila socked her in the left sand bag. She turned around, bent over at the waist and mooned the crowd at JR's. She gave us all the finger as she walked off stage. The winner was immediately forgotten. Even as she fiddled endlessly with her tits to make them point the right way after Lila's punch, nobody remembered there was another contestant.

I caught up with her outside hailing a cab. It was chilly that night and she stood down on the Landing, on the cobblestone street, dripping wet in the forty degree night.

"You're gonna catch a cold, Lila."

She turned and regarded me coolly, trying to remember if there was a reason I'd know her name. "Get lost perv." She turned her attention back to the cabs that weren't coming.

"I bet your name really is Lila, isn't it?"

"Why, you getting a tattoo?" She gave up on the corner and started to walk toward the north end and the casino. All the cabs waited by the Admiral for fares.

"Need a lift?"

She ignored me and kept walking.

Another couple of patrons stumbled out JR's side door and began to approach Lila from the cross street. They were college aged shitheads in sports shirts and jean shorts, with ball caps turned backward above their tan, booze-broadened faces. One of them, sporting a necklace of conch shells called out to her. "Hey, Surfboard show me your tits."

Lila didn't give them the satisfaction of even turning her head. She kept walking and disappeared around the corner. The two dudes walked in the same direction and I followed.

When I rounded the corner I saw they'd brought themselves up beside her, walking fast to match her pace. Conch shell's buddy with the blond goatee and Buffet Gut said to his friend, "It's a dude, Dude. I got bigger tits than him. Watch."

I'm not sure how far in the bag they already

were, but they either overestimated the effects of their charm or underestimated Lila's waifish volatility. When buffet gut reached out for the hem of her still wet t-shirt she grabbed the trespassing finger and broke it with a quick twist. On instinct he swung at her and she tore at his face with her tiny fingers and came away with blood colored nails.

Conch necklace came over his buddies' shoulder and smacked her high on her forehead with his fist. When Lila went down I saw red. The one asshole with angry red scrape marks across his face screamed at her calling her a bitch and promising to sue her or fuck her up or both. His buddy was giggling a little bit, glancing back and forth between his friend and Lila getting up slowly, braced against the wall. I walked up behind them and blindsided Conch Shell. Then I turned toward Buffet Gut and threw a hammer, pouring every ounce of advantage my extra fifteen years of alcohol thickening gave me, into his nose, which squished like a blood-swole tic. He never even knew I was there.

When I turned around, Lila was gone. I caught up to her down the street, wiping blood off her finger tips onto her white cotton shirt and by way of thanks;

she let me walk with her.

Trying to appear less winded than I really was, I sucked air through my nose and spit out in four blasts, "Where're you going? You shoulda won that contest, no doubt. It's a disgrace that you didn't. Just cause you're not blowing the owner every night."

She turned on her heel and looked me in the eye. "That true?"

I nodded while my heart rate returned to normal. When I was Lila's age, which I'd place in the late part of the twenties, I would still get in little scuffles most weekends, but I'd mellowed some in the years since. I told myself, like a fine wine. A fine, chubby wine with a steady job, my own apartment and car. "Everybody there was talking about it. JR's been bragging on it for a week now. Says she's got no technique, but lets him rub off between her tits. The gland canyon, he calls 'em."

"I knew it." She wagged her finger at me like she'd been trying to make this point for a long time, now. "I knew I coulda beat that peroxide bitch fair and square." Her hands rested on her hips. "You cheered for me?"

"That's a fact."

"What's your name?"

"Carl."

"Carl, you've got a car nearby?"

"Uh-huh."

"You wouldn't mind giving me a lift? My girlfriend deserted me."

"Sure. Where to."

"Wings down in South County. There's another contest at 11."

Turned out she'd been competing regularly. Most nights actually. Picked up prize money a couple times a week on average, which was saying something seeing as how she's not got the biggest rack or the prettiest face. What she had in spades was spunk.

I took her to the next bar and she didn't even make the top five, but I yelled myself hoarse for her and she noticed. I guess that's why she ended up back at my place that night.

So that's how things started.

* * *

Now jump forward just one month in time and she's yelling at me that I'd better not quit and that if I can't keep it up till she's finished than I'm just no use. I'm looking at her skinny, naked body coiled tight with concentration and a demonic determined cast to her eyes, a look that normally I would respond to with an eager rigidity. Only I'm not. Now I'm just sinking lower and lower into what may become a terminal depression.

* * *

She'd got far beneath my skin, in such a quick time. I'd never had a girlfriend before, let alone one like Lila. We sat around my apartment a lot, listening to old shitkicker music together and went to see bands all the time. At the Horton Heat show I even let her see me cry. She got a sad smile on her face and reached up to smear a tear across my face. When we got back to my place, I tipped my hand. I called it love.

And she hit me right away with a life plan that'd occurred to her recently.

The thought of having a baby was so weird. It didn't seem real. The thought of having one with Lila was like a dream and I was half convinced that that was all it was. Every lucid moment, though, I made plans for our future. I started reading books about pregnancy and how precious children were, which confused me some because all the kids I knew or grew up with were little shits from the get-go, but I was determined to do the fatherhood thing right.

I started looking for a better place to live out in the county, a little house to rent with a back yard. Maybe even get a dog. There was a supervisor position opening at the Walgreen's and I decided to throw my hat in the ring.

Rings were another thing on my mind and I found myself browsing the coupon section of the Sunday papers for Shane Company ads. I didn't like the idea of somebody calling my kid a bastard, but when I brought up getting hitched to Lila, the scary way her face twisted, youd've thought I'd suggested a three way with her mom. "Uh-uh, no. I don't want to ever get married, Carl."

"But why's that, Li?"

"It's cause is all, Carl. Gonna have to trust me on this one."

"But I love you Lila. We're gonna have a baby and I want to do this one thing right."

She pouted and put her hands on the sides of my face and looked up into my eyes. "Carl, honey, I want to have a baby too and I want you around to help and daddy it, but I don't wanna spoil what we got by getting the government involved, that's all. Nothing's changed and it's sweet, but…"

"What about a ring, then?"

"Pardon?"

"What would you say to just wearing a ring? I'd like to get you a ring and have you wear it."

At this she smiled big. "Carl, I would be happier than shit to wear your ring."

Good enough.

* * *

Flash forward one week and she's on top, sweaty and convulsing shouting orders to me. "Oh! Carl, ugh, get in there, uh, whew, all the way, uh, c'mon, harder, don't you dare pussy out on me you son of a bitch. Carl I swear to you if we don't make a baby tonight you and me are through."

That's pressure.

* * *

"Baby, guess what? I got us tickets to the Copernicus show at Pop's tomorrow night!" She looked excited like the quarterback just asked her to homecoming.

"Who's Copernicus?"

"You know, Copernicus – 'Ooh, woman, I'm the

one you don't know you want'." I didn't know the song, and her rendition didn't excite me much, but she sure enough looked eager to go.

"I don't know that song."

"Sure you do. They opened for Tesla and Mr. Big back about 1990 and my dad took me to see them." She put her hands into the back pockets of my trousers and rubbed herself up against my leg. "I remember that show was the first time I thought I wanted to try sex."

"Really?"

"Oh yeah, Tracy Collins was sooo hot. He had –"

"He?"

"Yeah, he. Tracy was, is the lead singer. He had gorgeous long, dark hair and didn't really have to wear make up to be pretty like everybody was those days." She went to the other room and began digging through a collection of cds she'd moved into my apartment last week.

This wasn't sounding good. "You mean he's one of those fairies with the teased out hair-dos and eyeliner used to prance around in music videos?"

"Yeah, but Tracy Collins was so much better than that."

Huh. Well, there didn't seem to be any way of getting around going without really letting Lila down. Besides, I was changing. Growing.

She came back into the room with a cd cover held out for my inspection. I took it and looked at the picture. Five skinny guys with their hair teased out using what must've been a whole can of spray, dressed in black cowboy boots and tight black jeans with scarves, hoop earrings and silky blouses open to their navels so that their downy soft chest hair could catch the light, smirked at me in front of a solid pink backdrop. I searched each smooth, rouged and mascara heavy face till I came to the one blowing me a kiss with sparkly pink colored lips.

Lila's finger reached over the top of the cd cover and rested just above the kiss blower. I looked over the top of the picture at her staring back at me expectantly with a finger in her mouth held delicately by her front teeth. She snatched her hand back and put it between her knees.

"You gotta be shittin me, Li."

A high pitched squeal was all the answer I got.

* * *

Flash forward to the next night and Lila's just

about to cry. She's pulling on the useless dick meat in her hands, her frustration matching my embarrassment. We're both exhausted and chaffed. There's a heavy smell of blood and shit hanging in the hotel room. I'm beginning to look around and think about leaving and Lila senses it. "No! We aren't through. I can't do this all by myself. Carl, you have to stay here and get me pregnant." And she loses it. The frustration and exhaustion is finally too much. She cries. It's the first time I've seen her vulnerable like this. Her face is red and puffy, her legs and ass just chapped and raw and I can't bear it.

"Okay, one more try, Lila. Just one more."

She nods, grateful, but can't stop sobbing while I stretch and flex, trying to work out some of the stiffness and ache from the last hour's efforts. I look into Lila's eyes shiny with tears and I reach over to smear them away.

I know I've already lost her.

* * *

On our way across the river to Pop's, the same place I caught Motorhead with Nashville Pussy not long ago, she's so excited that I'm convinced it's going to be a great time. One that we'll look back on fondly years from now. We'll tell the kid about it. Hell, we'll tell the kid about the night he was conceived. Lila said that tonight was the night, she was ovulating and she'd got us a hotel room for afterwards. She gave me a key.

When the first jangly acoustic strums of Capernicus's set cue the whistles and cheers from the faithful, I look up to see Lila's sex god, Tracy Collins, now middle aged, overweight and nearly bald, close his eyes in concentration and give that girly voice of his a push. What comes out is a beautiful and true note that shuts me right the hell up. I don't know if Lila knew his looks and body had gone, but she didn't show any signs of surprise or disappointment. It was me who wasn't prepared for him.

Number after number, Tracy fuckin Collins broke my heart with his voice, aged and cracked by cigarettes and over use, but finally as honest and lived in as Ty Crenshaw's Rickenbacker.

At the end of the set they do their signature number and I do recognize it. It was one of those songs that was just everywhere for six months somewhere between 1988 and 1992. I'd hated it. The lyrics seemed like meaningless saccharine sentiments strung together against a backdrop of acoustic guitars and a fuckin chamber orchestra with a blistering guitar solo stuck somewhere in the middle, but not tonight. Tonight it's something new. The guy singing it isn't some twenty year old pretty boy. He's got some life under his belt, some hard times and a long slide from the top to Pop's plus all the painful learning about yourself that goes with it.

When he hits the "It's gonna be alright, alright? Woman, alright?" bit which used to be my least favorite part, I can't take any more and head for the men's room. It's empty. Everybody is outside, mesmerized by the former clown up there singing the shit out of their expectations. I lock myself in a stall, sit down and begin to cry.

It starts off as shudders. Little convulsions that double me over, hugging myself and rocking on the toilet. There's a high pitched raspy moan leaking out of me that just intensifies until I'm sobbing and convulsing, helpless against the tide of bottled up emotion the little fairy in the blouse and eye make-up just uncorked. I stay in that stall a long fucking time.

Time to buy myself a dress.

* * *

Flash forward one hour and I'm seeing red. I kill the guy. Lila screams.

* * *

When I emerge from the bathroom the club has transformed. The house lights were up and AC/DC was on the system. Some of the members of Copernicus are sitting at tables along the back wall applying their signatures to old posters and t-shirts. I don't see Tracy Collins with them. I also can't find Lila.

I walk around for a few minutes scanning the thinned out crowd before abandoning my search of the inside and head for the parking lot. Right away I spot my own car with a note stuck under the wiper. It's from Lila instructing me to meet her at the diner down the street in an hour. She's got something special planned for me.

My already tender heart gives an especially soft thwump, thwump in my chest and I feel more tears coming. God, that Tracy Collins really fucked up my emotional equilibrium. But I let it happen, getting into the car for some privacy. Lila's so sweet. I love her so much and making a baby with her is just about the best thing that's ever gonna happen to me in my life.

I figure two can be romantical and go to the 7-11 for some paper roses. Thinking I'll spread them all over the hotel room so she'll be surprised and happy when we get there. The guy behind the counter smirks at me while I'm buying the flowers and a ten dollar bottle of wine. When I notice, he answers my unspoken question. "You see Copernicus tonight?"

"Yeah." And I realize I'd been humming their hit.

"I hate that song." He says while he's ringing up the sale and his abrasiveness throws a kink into my mood. "Everybody's humming that song tonight. It's gonna be stuck in my head for a week."

I'm angry at him, for shitting on my music, but at the same time, I understand 'cause I'd have felt the same way last night if someone had got that song stuck in my head. I just take my change and leave. I don't wanna start any shit.

I keep humming the song all the way to the hotel, even singing the words that I know under my breath. I smile at the lady behind the desk and hum my way down the hall with my flowers.

When I open the door to the room, I'm

immediately aware that I'm not alone. Slapping and grunting sounds hit me like a hammer and I drop the flowers. Quietly I close the door and creep around the corner where some fat asshole fucking Lila from behind on the bed.

My first thought is to rescue her from the rapist, but her vocal encouragement makes me reevaluate the situation. She's going uh, uh, oh yeah, yeah like that, right like that, uh, uh.

My whole world goes psychedelic in an instant. Spots burst bright red behind my eyes and the room goes away till all I can see is my sweet Lila fucking somebody else like I'm watching it in a fun house mirror. The shape of them moving together bubbles up and contracts, pulsing to a trippy rhythm and I feel like I'm going to fall down. But I don't. I go through my repertoire of emotions in a heartbeat and settle finally on rage.

There's an animal howl that gets all of our attention and it's only in retrospect that I realize it was me making the terrible sound. Lila and Tracy Collins turn their heads toward me, but it's too late. I swing that wine bottle right at his head.

Tracy had abused his body so severely for so

long, it was really a miracle that he'd lived long enough for me to kill him. But that single blow to the head was all it took and he collapsed on the bed, transformed in an instant from Lila's teenage sex god into a dead tub of shit.

Lila screamed. Not like a scaredy scream or even surprised, but angry beyond even what I'd felt when I did it. "No, you idiot, no. Asshole, fucking asshole what'd you do?"

* * *

Ty Crenshaw died. Tracy Collins died. Ty left behind a fortune and a string of bastards to inherit it. Tracy didn't have any wife. No children. Lila'd figured he was still worth something. And look at him. He wasn't going to live much longer.

When I'd told her I loved her, and she saw that it was true, it was like the aligning of all the right stars. She did want to raise a baby with me; she just didn't want me to sire the brat. And she didn't want me to know that I hadn't. She'd have been happy to use me as Mr. Mom for a year or two until Tracy Collins met his inevitable early end and then dump me and prove with a paternity test, her child's true father. Figured she could inherit some of that fortune he hopefully wouldn't have completely depleted.

But I'd fucked it up.

* * *

"What did I do, Li? What did you do? What the fuck did you do? Broke my fucking heart is all."

"He's dead, Carl."

"Looks that way, Li. Hope you're happy." We looked down at the body when it farted. "What the shit?"

She grabbed him under the arms and tried to tug him over the bed to a better spot. "Don't just stand there, help me."

"We need to get out of here, Li."

"Uh-uh, I'm getting pregnant tonight and now you've gotta help me."

"What are you talking about? If you think I'm gonna give you a baby now, you're so wrong." But she wasn't listening to me. Instead she was taking Tracy's still rigid dick in her hands and beginning to straddle the dough boy. "The hell are you doing, Lila? That's sick."

"C'mon, we can still make this work, but you're going to have to help me."

"What?"

She turned her face to me and the fierceness behind her eyes set an ice block squarely in my stomach. "He wont last that much longer. You've got to make him cum."

Her theory, which I had my doubts on, but wasn't about to voice, was that he could be made to ejaculate by milking the prostate. I didn't know it at the time, but it's true that a man can be brought to orgasm by sticking a finger or two up his ass and rubbing the prostate gland. Homos do it, but they don't always use a finger, and I guess any dude can do it to his own self if he wanted to, but as far as the method's merits on the recently deceased go, I really couldn't say.

I guess I still loved her.

She'd used me and cheated on me and probably would've laughed about it later, but she still held a special place in my heart. I had changed. Grown. Somewhere in the midst of all that reading I'd done on parenting a critter and taking care of both child and mother, I'd realized that my priorities had changed. I wasn't living just for myself any more. Lila was my priority and soon our kid would be too. I'd gotten used to it pretty quickly, such was the hold she had on me.

So, I guess I still loved her. It's the only reason I can think of that I went along with her plan. It was hard work, let alone disgusting, but Lila coached me and all I had to do was concentrate on her voice and command. And follow.

I got underneath him and with the help of a bottle of Astro-glyde, worked my fingers up his butt and started rubbing away while she ground into him from above. He was heavy and unwieldy. His head flopped backward onto my shoulder and I buried my face in what was left of his hair, preferring to smell the sweat and shampoo there than the sex and death scents that were rapidly overpowering everything else.

My hand cramped up and I had to switch back and forth between right and left several times. Lila bucked and twitched like a pro, her eyes shut tight mostly, but opening to transfix me every few minutes. Time melted away. My hands were covered in blood and shit.

Still Lila worked at it.

I realized finally that I was truly outmatched by her. However much I changed and grew, I would never be able to equal her in a relationship. We were driven by different forces. She was beyond me in every way.

And as I watched her doggedly press on, I knew two things simultaneously. One was that however this turned out, Lila would survive. She'd move on and be just fine. And two, it was over between us.

The Whole Buffalo

Right from the start, the papers made such a big deal of it, but the whole thing was really blown way out of proportion. Not to say they got it wrong, exactly, but certainly many of the details were sensationalized. Can't really blame them for trying, though. The Hamilton County Gazette's a bit starved for readership. I've know them to reprint some stories from previous issues to fill space sometimes. Nobody ever complains about that. Not sure anybody else notices. Anyhow, it was a big deal to them to get a story picked up for the nationals. The good days dried up pretty quick, though as the big guys with field reporters and budgets and the like just sent their own folks to St. Thomas to excavate what story there was and then, like the vultures they are, leave the town, to rot, stripped to a pile of bones, and then they're off to follow the next salacious tale in some other nook of the world.

The Gazette's editors still saw a healthy bump in readership and advertising for a few months and when the trial came about, they experienced it again, armed this time with a certain worldliness and know how, they were short of before. For instance they learned there are loaded words you can toss in to any sentence and instantly you've got a headline: mutilate... corpse... cannibal...

I never wanted the attention, but I'm a good sport. I knew that it was my chance to pump a little money into the tax base of the town. So I played along, granted interviews, held back some of my best stuff for the local boys, though they were often pretty slow on the uptake, and I had to spoon feed them and answer questions they weren't asking. I'd like to think I maybe paid for some road work or uniforms for the football team. Can't hardly have a town worth living in around here without a high school football team. Building block of society, really. I was not and am not ashamed of anything I did, but you'd have thought I was a real sicko, if the papers were your only source of information. You'd have thought I was some demented, old necrophile jack off, but what it really boiled down to was thriftiness and good business sense. Like the Indians, you know? Use the whole buffalo.

The other day, a reporter asked me and I couldn't give a grand total. You think I kept books on that? No sir. Whatever I may be, stupid is not one of my traits. Though, I've not thought much as to volume, I have wondered occasionally if all the families with junk stored at the Stock 'N Lock had any notions that it was hallowed ground they tread, or if they had familial connections to anyone resting in peace behind one of my garage doors. Now that I've got nothing but time on my hands, I suppose I could put my mind to some calculations and arrive at a figure shortly. It would be approximate mind you, but I will, now that I think of it, try to.

Maybe get us a gift shop, build a tourism industry.

What really does wrinkle my scrotum, though, is that nobody would have any problem with the whole affair at all if it weren't for that insufferable bitch Susie Dross. That uptight boner killer nearly took down the whole town, in the end. Just about killed it as surely as if she'd set a fire or used an atom bomb. I was the one who finally put an end to the old biddy, humanely even, much better than she deserved, and do I get a medal?

Let's just say none of us get what we deserve.

Susie Dross had a husband, you might say, though I wouldn't. I've been one before and let me tell you, any emasculation I may have suffered at the hands of my various ex's would merely feel like tight pants compared to the continual and public nut flaying Herbert Dross took up as his daily cross. She may as well have kept his testes tied to either end of a baton and twirled the motherfucker in front of a brass band everywhere they went together. He may have had his esophagus clawed out of his neck by the pack of dogs that ran wild in the woods on the south side of town, but I haven't ruled out suicide. I don't know what exactly you'd call that relationship, but marriage just doesn't seem right.

Anyway, after the attack Susie brings her funeral business my way and I really thought about turning her down from the outset. I didn't because that's not something I've made a practice of in thirty years of service as a mortician. Donnelly Funeral Home has lain to rest St. Thomas's dead for most of a hundred years now. When I bought out the Donnelly family back in 1978, they'd been the first and most trusted name in death care in all of Hamilton County and they didn't accomplish that by turning away clients based on personal dislike.

So one night, as I'm standing over the sink with my micro-waved enchiladas not even thinking about how empty the house is these days, there is a knock at the door, which I'm accustomed to. I suck the insides out at the back end where they're threatening to drip, then set down my dinner on a paper plate nearly transparent with grease, suck my fingertips and wipe them on my pants, donning my black jacket as I go for the front entrance. My stomach drops into my gonads when I see that it's Susie Dross all barely composed and puffy on my doorstep.

"Good evening, Mrs. Dross." I say, like she were any other human person I might have reason to see at my house.

"No. No Mr. Wainscot, it is not." She sniffles just

a bit and touches a well used kerchief to her face. "Herbert..." And she breaks into a fit of tears as violent as it is short. I stand solemnly quiet before her, waiting for the news. "Mr. Dross has been killed this very evening." And she waits there for me to supply the appropriate professional, if not personal, condolences.

Good for him, is my first thought. I can't believe he lasted this long, is my second. "I'm so sorry for your loss." is what pours from my lips, like some automaton set perpetually on polite. I hold open the door for her, and she enters.

I lead her to my consultation room, just off the vestibule, straight ahead as you enter. It features decor the very substance of sobriety and sincerity, picked out by Tamara Donnelly, grandmother to those I bought the place from, all those years ago. It's been a good choice to leave it alone and not redecorate as each of my wives has encouraged me to do over the years. People seem to find something reassuring in the old fashioned look of the place. I often think, as I lead the grieving into this 19th century time warp how shocked most of their delicate sensibilities would be if they knew the acts committed upon the furniture on which they now rest. I can't speak for the Donnelly's, but it is my experience that the dark tones of the wood paneling and carpet and the dim lighting have remained there just as much to cover the various stains crusted in to the fibers and left on the walls as to assure them they are in the best and most respectful and understanding of hands.

In this very room my first wife and I used to throw parties with couples from out of town. Cool little get-togethers with some costumes and coke. There'd be all manner of role play and experimentation. We were always careful not to include locals, because you never know who's going to get the heebie-jeebies discussing the details of a loved one's funeral sitting upon the very couch they watched you pork her on. Wearing the bunny ears.

Learned a lot about ourselves as a couple and individuals, which I always thought was a good thing, but that was where I just saw the world different from Joni. Eventually something really freaked her out, got her permanently out of the mood and into the booze. She sulked and cussed me good, and took to saying some pretty hurtful things on a pretty regular basis. I told her finally to cut that shit out and she was ready to. I think she joined a cult or something.

Susie Dross has recovered her composure by the time I've placed the lacquered tissue box on the solid oak coffee table in front of her. The sturdiness of the furniture is another reason I've not redecorated. You come to appreciate good craftsmanship after collapsing a couple Ikea pieces of crap just trying to get your nob polished. She seems completely back to her stern old self, and I just want to get this over with. "Mr. Wainscot, my husband deserves the very best."

A martyr's remembrance 'is what I think.

"And I expect you will not take his meager pension into consideration when you make your recommendations for the service." I can tell she's really going to get off on her new opportunity to suffer nobly. "You needn't worry about such things. If he's left me only enough to cover the ceremony, I'm sure that God has put that before me for a reason."

She just can't resist taking digs at him, even in her grieving. He never made enough money, is what I'm supposed to hear, so I'm perfectly capable of fending for myself in his absence, the way I have had to my whole life. The blame is really on me for marrying a man of such low quality and character as to not care enough to provide better for me and then to just check out and leave me with nothing.

I squeeze my fists a couple of times, just to get some tension out. She bothers me. She senses the devil about me, I know from loose talk I've picked up from other clients over the years. Plus those fiery editorials she prints in the papers have made it pretty clear the type of people who earn her contempt. St. Thomas is a pretty small town though, and unless she wants to drag her ass, with the broom handle poking out, over the state line and create a lot more hassle in paperwork and legalities, Donnelly Funeral Home will be providing her the sensible, assuring and steady support she'll need to weather this storm.

"Mrs. Dross, let me assure you that I take this period in a family's life very seriously and would suggest in your case, just as in every case brought before me, modesty in scale and arrangement." I can see she wants me to notice her irritation at this remark. Nobody comes in asking for the cheapest crate we got, and I'm glad enough to play this role and offend their pride until they come around to my reasoning. Before she can offer a token rebuttal, I continue. "Frankly Mrs. Dross, nothing speaks of a guilty conscience louder than a garish funeral. Just like the most elaborate weddings always produce the shortest marriages. People see through that, and I know that is not the impression you would want them to have. Certainly, I am not suggesting that a guilty conscience resides in you, but I am quite serious when I say that, that is how it will look if you insist on silk pillows, printed announcements or other silly, ornamental things just because some huckster with a black suit and a pinched sincerity about him says it is the best."

She sits there with both hands in gloves that reach nearly to her elbows and pressed tightly between her thighs which are quivering just a little bit under the strain of composure and it reminds me of this oriental chick who had sat right there once, in the same spot and with exactly the same posture, except the gloves were the only thing she was wearing. It's spooky, really these little coincidences in life. It has me wondering if Mrs. Dross is leaving a damp spot on the chair like old Miss Saigon did. Somehow, I doubt it. What I don't doubt is that if there is anyone in St. Thomas who could pick up the acrid scent of the chair beneath the basic aroma of the house, and form a quick opinion as to origin, it's Susie Dross.

She looks up finally, which if she were oriental I'd take to mean she'd finished peeing and says "You are the professional here, Mr. Wainscot. Herbert is only the first husband I have lost. I will take your opinion under advisement. I will insist, however on an open casket."

* * *

Back in the late seventies, it seemed like a pretty good idea to buy out the Donnellys. It was not such a bummer, to live here then, especially if you knew a thing or two about textiles or construction. The population had grown steadily for ten years thanks to romantic notions of small communities surrounded by nature and outside the watchful eye of the government. Things were looking up. There were new businesses starting all the time. The Syam pet food factory opened up and created a lot of jobs, and by 1980 there were rumors we had a K-Mart coming too. But Reaganomics were right around the corner like a blue Monday and fuck if the whole town didn't go in the toilet.

By the end of the eighties, the textile plant had closed. The union had had its ass handed to it by a bunch of ten year olds in Asia. Most of the mom and pop spots had gone tits up and the population had dwindled to an all time low. The baby boom that had been perched on the horizon, throwing off fierce fuck me vibes, like the class slut just dying to get it on with the whole death care industry, picked up and moved out of town. Those that were left, were them with deep roots, like Herb and Susie Dross or without the means or inclination to get out, like me.

I was being quit by wife number two at the time. I had a receding hair line and just enough soft to me to seem comfortable, but underneath I was angry. Pissed off at the demise of the place and my marriage. Patty said I was a small time dreamer and a big time pervert and should stay here and rot. She wanted nothing to do with me, or St. Thomas. The blow of a second failed marriage made me determined to stick it out and make a go of it, with the business. Can't say as to why. I just hated to lose, I guess.

There were a few other like minded business men in town. Hunter Malcomson who owned the Syam plant and Walt Grimaldi who had one of the best livestock farms in Hamilton County were friends of mine and comrades of sorts having served on local councils and committees together and frequenting the same bordellos. It was the three of us who struck the deal that kept the place from dying completely.

Thanks to our determination and innovation, the town lived on and as the nineties were coming to a close, our little hamlet was experiencing growth again for the first time in twenty years. The new comers were hippies or burnouts ducking trouble created elsewhere, but young for the most part and some were starting families, eager to trade the sag and depression of urban poverty for the real thing out in the sticks.

* * *

I got to the hospital later that night to pick up the body. The orderly helping me with the gurney says "Holy shit, he's a big son of a bitch." straining as we begin to ascend the ramp to the hearse. And he's right. Herb Dross is heavy. Not fat, but solid and really really tall. Like 6'7" or more. His humongous feet hang off the end of the gurney along with his ankles and a good four inches of leg and the muscles in my arms begin to ache a little in anticipation.

"Show some respect for the dead." I say as a joke, but he doesn't get it. Must be new. Driving him back to the home, it strikes me I never realized how large he was. Somehow that little bit of a thing he was married to had shrunk him using only the voodoo of her glare and behavior. She'd nearly completely disappeared him, this giant of a man. I pictured him dissolving into the atmosphere like a seltzer tablet, just like I'd want to, every time she'd send back meals or return clothing, because nobody made them right. And I'd seen him dissipate before my eyes while she talked loudly to herself at the grocery store, disgusted by the magazines and concerned for the children forced to stand in front of them while mommy bought the food. I'm sure Herb caught shit from all sides any time after she'd attended public meetings or had a letter to the editor published in the Gazette bemoaning the crumbling pillars of society - chivalry, decency and patriotism.

Why he never left her, is beyond me.

"Nobody will say you took the coward's way if you killed yourself, Herb." I toast him with a shot of Jameson from my flask, driving past the dog food plant, now. I picture him spreading peanut butter on his throat and going for a walk in the woods or wearing t-bone steaks strapped underneath his clothes all the time, just waiting for his lucky day, and it all reminds me of a joke. "Stop me if you've heard this one, Herb. You know how to make a dog stop humping your leg?"

He has no idea.

"Suck his dick." I say and crack myself up nearly sending whiskey through my nostrils, which burns like the clap.

* * *

Never did attend a business class in my life. In my day it wasn't always the way to get a tinfoil stamp to vouch for your competence any damn time you wanted to do any damn thing. Kids these days, I don't know how they do it, spending half their life in schooling, all blue balled until they've got a certificate for the permission to finally go ahead and try something maybe they're not all that hot to anymore. All to say, maybe if I had, I could explain the economics of my reasoning to you better, if I'd been to some fancy pants school with the stamps and all, but the easiest I know how is: burying people costs money. For the coffin, for the plot and for the digging for starters. Displaying a dead body in a box is really where you make your margin in my game.

When they started snooping around last year and that first batch of corpses they found in the basement, neatly stacked behind the curtain, was getting all the media attention, you were maybe shocked. But I'd bet there were more than a few of you later, when they opened all the storage units and found some of the others, who said to yourself, "There's a shrewd business man.", with something like a smile in your tone.

Trust me, the dead don't care whether they're hot or cold, in the dark or light, bone in or nugget style. That's one of the main perks of death. You get one complaint out of any corpse ever entrusted to me, and I'll refund every nickel I ever made. And as far as the living are concerned, what they don't know is what they pay me for. Everybody was much better off before Susie Dross noticed that the legs of her dear departed husband didn't terminate in feet any longer and threatened to go make such a high holy stink of it all.

The orderly had been right. The son of a bitch was big. Too big in fact for my coffins. Either of them.

THE WHOLE BUFFALO

Now before you get all indignant over this point, let me just ask if you've ever slept a night in a hotel? My friend, I'm not sure exactly what you did in yours, but there's some people, called everybody else in the whole damn world, who went ahead and got their freak on.

Patty used to enjoy hotels. Big ones, little ones, rattraps and luxury suites. If it had mini bar and a porno box, all the better, but really any spot she could go and let down her hair, away from the familiarity of home, with all the baggage and responsibility of it soaked in to the atmosphere, she became a wild one. I hope they boil the sheets. I saw a TV show, not long back where they took some of that CSI equipment into a bunch of different hotels of differing cost to the consumer, to see what evidence had collected in each room over the years. To a one, they looked like Jackson Pollack had jizzed all over the ceiling and walls and bedspread, when they turned on that infrared light. Just shot some world record size loads with stupefying trajectories at mysterious targets.

And that's where you stayed.

So, yeah I re-used my coffins. Big deal. Not like my bodies are lining the walls with fluids and even if they were, it's not like the next one would mind. Again, what the living don't know, all the details of body draining and dressing and disposing? That's what they pay me for. So just pay me already and don't go micro-managing every little thing.

Susie Dross, at the service, goes up to the coffin and it is open casket, just like she insisted upon. I've put the poor bastard's face and throat back together with glue and given him make up to look like a real life wooden doll. And everybody says how peaceful he looks, how at peace he seems and all manner of bullshit about peace. Everyone, that is, except the widow.

She's so distracted, she can't cry, can't let all that emotion go. These services are for the living to experience catharsis in communal demonstrations of grief and, just like an orgy, if one person's not committed it can throw off everyone else. It's a group effort. Without complete cooperation, when just one person is holding back, you become self-conscious, notice maybe how silly you look and it all goes to shit. And Susie - how could you cut off my dead husband's feet with a hack saw? - Dross is not getting the ball rolling with a little sniffle.

It's awkward. She just keeps shooting glances over at the coffin, like it had spoken to her. The minister goes on about dust to dust and I say amen in my mind to that, and Mrs. Dross, had she a squeak in her neck, could not have been more conspicuous, turning her head back and forth between the preacher and the casket.

When the service finally closes and nobody has said a thing and everyone else has left, Susie comes marching back in, as I'm lowering the lid. My balls trade places as I anticipate whatever unpleasant pleasantry she's about to loose on me.

"A lovely service." I offer reflexively.

She doesn't acknowledge that I've said anything. "Open it." she says plainly, like she knows I'll do whatever she asks.

"Maam?" I say. She is probably ten years younger than me, but has been a maam in my book since I've known her.

"Open the casket. I want to see my husband."

"Please excuse me for saying so, Mrs. Dross, but the body in there is no longer your husband. He doesn't really look like the man you were married to because, he's dead and no amount of concealer or rouge is going to-"

"Open the casket or I will call the police."

"Of course." So, I do. Herb Dross, made up like a Ziggy Stardust harlequin doll, looks up at heaven only to see Susie standing over him, grim and disapproving once again. Give the poor guy a break I think, and I'm not sure if I'm referring to the departed or myself.

"Open the other end."

"I'm sorry, Mrs. Dross, but the other end doesn't-"

"I want to see his feet."

Here it comes. That was not the first time I'd had to trim some off the stems to get the deceased to fit. What can I say? It makes better sense than buying a brand new casket for every single body. You have any idea how much that would cost? There was of course the one I had to replace after Barb, my third wife, broke it. She had a thing for doing it in tight spaces. When the broom closets became too cavernous, we quickly graduated to coffins, most of them empty. Again we come back to that quality and craftsmanship issue. I think the spill had heightened the experience for her because we finished before collecting what's-his-nuts off the floor and propping him up in the corner where he would be out of the way. He looked as if he were a night watchman, drunk on the job. Of course, after that, it was like he was watching and she had to have another go. Then that became a new thing.

Herb Dross's feet were still in the freezer. I think.

So, I quit stalling and open the other end. His slacks are hemmed to not bunch around his shoes, which are fastened to the stumps beneath the pants. She stares at them a few interminable seconds before grabbing a shoe.

It comes off, empty in her hand.

* * *

Nobody missed her for a couple of days. She was an intensely solitary person, an irony considering her insistence at knowing everyone else's business and printing it in the news paper. She had many informational sources, but none could really be called friends. There had been a small turn out for the funeral service, but no one was invited to the burial. It was to be private.

No heads turned when she missed the school board meeting. Everyone was probably relieved by her absence, though her failure to notify the board in advance, must've sat uneasily on a few minds. It was her conspicuous missing of First Lutheran's nine a.m. service and subsequent truancy at the eleven o'clock, which raised eyebrows.

When the sheriff finally put out a missing person's report, she'd been dead nearly a week. The sheriff came by to speak to me. I was expecting that. He said no one had seen Susie Dross since the funeral and I nodded my head solemnly and said I'd heard that too.

"Far as I can figure it, you'd be the last person to see her around these parts." There was no accusation in his voice, so I was relaxed.

"Really? She have family anywhere?"

"Looking in to that, but we haven't found any yet. She and Herb grew up here, had no kids or siblings and parents are deceased on both sides, but we're looking for uncles aunts and cousins. Did she seem unusually upset to you, Mr. Wainscot?"

"No, not that I noticed, sheriff. Of course she was upset, but I wouldn't say unusually so."

"Some folks have said she seemed distressed during the service. Did she mention anything that may have been bothering her?"

Did she ever not? seemed like the appropriate response, but I let it go unsaid.

"Yes. She didn't like the job I'd done putting old Herb's face back together. I tried to convince her to have a closed casket, but you know how she was, sheriff, when she got an idea. I told her I wasn't a miracle worker, but she insisted and I thought I did a remarkable job, myself. Probably most others in attendance would say I had too, but, and not to speak ill of the grieving, you know what she was like."

He took it all in, considered it and looked as if he was satisfied. "Alright, then, you have a good day."

"You too, sheriff."

* * *

Any type of business you run creates waste. It's just the nature of things. The trick to success is managing it so that it doesn't devour your profits. If you're really good, sometimes you can turn that waste into a byproduct that can be used.

Syam pet food didn't compete with the big boys, but they did have a good little regional game. Hunter bought all of the meats from local farmers. Walt Grimaldi's farm was his main source. Everyone had felt the pinch of the times and those with pride in local products and services held Hunter, Walt and myself in high regard. We'd made a go of it in the face of big business and globalization. Success like ours came from smarts, commitment and innovation.

Because of our small size, the mechanics of it was simpler than you'd think. I have no staff. I'm a one man show, so there were no unwanted eyes seeing things they'd rather not, when I'd bring a delivery Walt's way. Likewise, Walt was a small business man and did his own slaughtering, always had. I wont lie to you and say the first time wasn't weird. There was a sort of distance created between the three of us that night that remained to the end, but our arrangement stood and though I didn't see the two of them outside of town business anymore, I can't say I'd take it back.

Like I mentioned before, I've always thought that any sort of self knowledge you can gain is good. I feel it's important to know your own capabilities and limitations and embrace your true identity, to make the most of this life, but some folks just aren't happy when they meet the real them, as if life were some meddlesome friend setting them up on a blind date with themselves. Some people just go for the appetizers, but I wanted desert, coffee and a night cap. By then I'd been working with the dead more than fifteen years, so the sight of them didn't bother me, but Walt and Hunter had to get pretty drunk to start carving.

The first was Mrs. Dunlevy, a batty old broad who'd passed on in her sleep at the retirement home. She'd outlived the last of her progeny and had no one to claim her, so we agreed she was a perfect first attempt. As per our agreement, all three of us had to be present for the inaugural run. We all had to get our hands dirty together, so to speak. I'd already fractured several laws just by bringing the body as had Walt by welcoming me on to his property with Edith Dunlevy in tow, so it was Hunter who had first go at her.

Walt strung her up by her ankles over the drain in his slaughterhouse. It was cold in there by necessity, but we were, all three, sweating profusely. She swung there for a few moments, wrinkled and purple like a five foot, eighty pound vulva. Her skin had a tough, leathery look to it, but proved to be more like paper when Hunter drew the blade across her gullet, like Walt had demonstrated. He'd done so and then promptly puked. It set off a chain reaction of vomiting that ended with the two of them emptied, on all fours in the gore, heaving globs of spit on to the floor and mixing with the blood, but like I said, the dead don't bother me. A few slugs of whiskey later, all that pansy shit was behind us.

Walt had taken the next cut himself. While she was still suspended, he used a curved carver to open her from the top of her privates all the way to the opening that Hunter had made. It took a bit of tugging, but that knife was a sharp fucker and he'd completed the cut in about thirty seconds. There was a rush of organs and her bowels slipped out like a can of fishing worms. Little pieces of this or that amateurs like to think they can identify, because they passed a high school class, dropped out around our feet.

After Walt cut all that away and took the hose to the floor good, she hung there halved, her shoulders were near touching in the back, and I thought the protrusion of her dark nipples looked something like the far set eyes of a hammer head shark. When she'd dripped out and Walt hoisted her over the table and let her down, that thin skin of hers had torn off where the chains had held her and there was exposed bone most of the way around, when the shackles were removed.

I held out my right hand and Walt gave me what I needed. The cleaver was heavy and un-retractable in my grip. It made for a therapeutic swing once I got the hang of it. Took off the head first and it required a surprising six tries to completely sever. I'd wanted to do this sort of work before and had on a couple occasions after a hard day, blown off some steam by letting loose on the mid section of someone I was charged with preparing. Just a few wild swings or jabs the results of which were easily concealed beneath suits or dresses that they'd wear till they rotted off. Still, it's not like I had something as gratifying as this cleaver to work with. All the instruments I had were designed for precision cutting and trimming and though I'd occasionally gone out to the garage for something a bit more savage, the best I'd come back with was a hammer and it pulverized bones - not as easily concealed as the cuts.

After her head had finally popped off and rolled away from the hold my left hand had on her chin, pushing it back for better leverage and access, there was a euphoric wave that enveloped me. My fingertips tickled with power and the sudden erection I had was impossible to conceal. Immediately I gripped the right arm at the elbow and slammed home a beauty of a blow just beneath the shoulder and the whole thing nearly broke completely off. Hunter Malcomson repeated, "Oh my god. Oh my god. Oh my god." over and over as I worked. As soundtracks go, it was not bad at all.

After her head, I saw to the other limbs in turn, each taking fewer and fewer attempts to separate. I was disappointed, truthfully when Walt insisted on taking over after that. I felt pretty damn good and it still brings back some tingly sensation in my gut, as I recall it now. Walt went to work and I took the Jameson from Hunter's hands. He was regarding me with a slack holding of his mouth and wide, unblinking fashion of eyes. He continued to ogle me for a while, but I wasn't bothered. I sat down against the wall, sweaty and exhilarated, happy to be amongst friends.

The next drink I took was the finest of my life. There was a warmth without burn that spread through my gut and in to my extremities until I was sure I glowed. As the tough bits of flesh began to fall off and collect beneath our feet, like rubbery, dry snow, the high pitched sound of Walt's electric saw sounded like the humming of birds and I slept with that song in my ears for a week.

If we were trying to pull this off, selling to restaurants or some fine foods line, it could be a problem, but what goes into pet food is what doesn't go in to yours. Hunter had to have a paper trail to show a supply line, but Walt had livestock and those heifers squeezed out critters like toothpaste. Who was gonna argue he was supplying more than he produced?

Maybe it was dramatic and over reaching for me to claim we'd saved the town single handedly, but we'd taken strides toward ensuring locally owned businesses didn't go belly up. I got half of what Hunter paid Walt for the meat, which was half of what he paid for the rest. Everybody saved money, everybody made money. Syam didn't have any lay offs, Grimaldi made an extra quarter in profits, and I was saving all kinds of costs and pulling in extra cash on top.

Of course there's some bodies that are of no use for meat. They've been embalmed or had chemo, more and more of that, these days sad to say. Still, I'm not going to get a shiny new box for each or put them into the ground. Especially not after my eyes were opened. What's no good for money, is worth ten times that in pleasure. I bought myself a good solid cleaver like Walt's and some heavy duty saws for the hell of it. If any of my wives were around to testify, they'd say I was a calmer, milder man today. I'd tell them I was in therapy.

* * *

When Barb bailed, I just quit marriages. The more receptive I got to her voyeuristic inclusion of our "guests", the less she seemed to enjoy it, as if the whole point of their presence was my discomfort. When I went so far as to mildly suggest one time disrobing a young couple who'd bought it together taking a dangerous bend on a rainy night, she decided it wasn't her bag anymore. I wasn't sure if it was the lady victim's undeniable attractiveness making her jealous or the full extent of the trauma they'd suffered on impact made apparent once they were nude that cooled her libido, but that was the last time. That night she couldn't sleep. She said she had to leave me and it had all been a terrible mistake. She decided she'd had enough of self discovery all together.

The note she left was designed to point an incriminating finger at me. It didn't spare any details of her own involvement and she seemed to have an undercurrent of self loathing I'd been completely unaware of, our entire relationship. She even went so far as to say she'd become involved with me on a dark whim to risk the borders she sensed I would push her beyond and I really was shocked to learn that. It was as honest an expression I'd ever heard from her.

Had she mailed it to someone or sent out some sort of evidence somewhere, I suppose it would have been disastrous, but as her actions seemed to be spontaneously conceived and passionately executed, she just didn't think it through that far. I own a mortuary after all.

She was high as a kite when she'd done it, but that didn't erase the admiration I felt for her conviction when I found her. Most ladies who attempt to check out with a razor blade and a bottle of sherry survive with little scratch marks, delicately placed at the base of the palms, and everybody knows that is not the way to do it. In some circles, I'm told, those little white marks are ornamental and something akin to a status symbol. Not for my Barb, though. She'd taken our best kitchen knife and made deep incisions from elbow to wrist with only a single hesitation cut that only went halfway. Then to make sure she'd finished the job, she'd drawn it straight through the fleshy bit under her first chin, tracing the outline of her jaw bone.

She looked for all the world like a pornographic novelty pez dispenser packaged in the bathtub. The note was left on top of her dresser.

She wasn't on to all of my practices. Obviously she knew I wasn't a straight arrow, what with her sexual proclivities so readily obliged, but the business end she was unaware of. Seems she would have mentioned them in the note had she known.

That I had a bad track record with women was common knowledge around town, so it came as no surprise when word got around that wife number three had left. Abandoned the marriage for parts unknown and good riddance.

I got on best I could. I got some hobbies. I found that I loved walks in the woods and I enjoyed feeding scraps from my personal stash to the dog pack out there. I was not daft enough to feed them out of my hand, but I'd leave packages and enjoy discovering their disappearance the next day. I also walked with a gun. You'd be crazy not to, like old Herb Dross.

Barb had been the first human flesh they'd tasted as far as I know. I had lovingly carved up her breasts and portions of her buttocks and thighs and a couple other fleshy cuts, marinated them overnight, then cooked them for ten hours in the slow cooker. I'd thought it would be maybe a highly romantic gesture to eat her myself.

It wasn't.

That much was obvious after a few bites. I was working on what was probably her tongue, judging by the tough chewiness it retained even after so long in the pressure cooker when I gave up and mourned in a more traditional way.

I still felt she should be eaten, or more precisely, consumed, absorbed in to another living thing. The poetic quality of the notion was not overwhelmed by the failure of practice. So over the course of the next several days, I fed her a piece at a time to the dogs in the woods. There were only a few at that time, but over the years they've grown in number and become more dangerous and even aggressive. Barb was the only one I cooked for them, but I found I enjoyed feeding the dogs too much to stop.

* * *

The late autumn air was crisp and exhilarating, with the smell of a wood burning fire working not far off. I was reverentially silent on my walk, but inside I was singing or at least humming a spirited tune. Over the weeks, I'd replayed the dispatching of Susie Dross many times to undiminishing pleasure in my mind. It made me feel for the first time in a long while, like I'd made a real contribution.

Over the years, the business had begun to feel like a meaningless exercise in survival, as banal and routine as going to the grocery store. It was no longer interesting or exciting. The town looked to have pulled out of its funk and maybe I wasn't so essential to its well being any more. I'd even given thought to the possibility of selling out and travelling for a while. But dispatching Mrs. Dross was something I could feel good about myself for and maybe there were others that I could eliminate the same way and be performing a useful societal function.

THE WHOLE BUFFALO

I was kidding myself if I thought I was going to be able to keep this game up long. Walt died of a massive coronary last year and Hunter had taken the opportunity and dissolved our partnership and friendship. I was just stockpiling bodies now. It was compulsive. What I was saving in burial costs, I was investing in refrigeration units and storage lockers.

Maybe it was far fetched. I thought there were numerous uses I would stumble on to for them. But, in truth, that prospect didn't hold the same appeal to me, it once did. Don't get me wrong, I enjoyed feeding the dogs. I felt more like one of them than any citizen in town, but they didn't even need me. It was not exactly what I'd call a reason to live. Pretty soon, I was going to have to start burying people or leave. If I was going to go, the idea of taking another nuisance like Susie with me deserved consideration.

It was Mrs. Dross that I was scattering to the beasts of the field on that November afternoon. I was down to the last of her. In an attempt to give Herb a break, I was careful to put him at the opposite end of the woods. My hope and fantasy was that the dog that ate Herb would sniff out and kill the ones who got Susie. That he'd go on some savage rampage and give her the karmic butt-fucking she had coming.

I had heard many shots echoing through the hills over the course of my stroll. It was rifle season after all. There was a particularly concentrated source of shooting south of me and I put off finishing my walk, not wanting to go into an area that heavily populated and trigger happy.

He startled me when he spoke and I cursed out loud. "Shit. You scared me, Hal."

"Sorry Mr. Wainscot. Shoot any dogs?"

The question struck me as sarcastic and I answered in kind, "Oh yeah, love to shoot dogs. Don't you?"

I was surprised at the reaction the comment had on his face. He looked slapped, but recovered a look of neutrality quickly and nodded curtly and said he would see me later, then continued walking.

It wasn't until I came across the first dog carcass that it dawned on me he was not being sarcastic at all. The feral beast was a big one, splayed on it's back, it's right front leg nearly separated from its torso by what looked to be a shotgun blast. Many smaller wounds pocked him, his white fur making them easy to find. Poor fella probably took several minutes to bleed out,

I thought. Must've been caught between a hunter and his life. Strange, too, I thought. These dogs were good at avoiding them.

The second one was still alive, though barely. I came across him five minutes later, lying on his side on the rise of a small hill amongst the nearly bare trees. His eyes followed me, but he lacked the strength to turn his head as I passed. He was past the point of whimpering and I would have thought him dead already, but for the steam escaping between ever lengthening pauses from his nose. The ground was covered in a thick mass of leaves and I suspected were he to be picked up, the undercarriage would be very bloody, but from where I stood, there was little to recommend him as mortally wounded, save for the small hole between his ribs trickling a dark substance, not pooling beneath him, but trailing into the leaves to disappear. That and the previously discovered dead colleague. I approached him cautiously and saw he had been shot at close range and by a more precise instrument which meant that indeed someone was shooting dogs today and they were more than one.

A panic began to rise in me with mysterious origin almost as if it were I being hunted down. My pace quickened as I walked toward home. I saw three more expired dogs on the return trip and each heightened the excitement increasingly threatening to overrule my senses. My gait widened with every sharp crack that reverberated over the hills and by the time I got back, I was in a dead run. I shut the door behind me and sank to the floor unable to pinpoint what exactly my anxiety was. After twenty minutes, I got to my feet and went to the kitchen where I splashed my face and neck with water before filling a glass from the sink and draining it down my throat three times. Then I switched to Jameson.

That night I slept with the Winchester beside me and in the morning I took it to the kitchen where I was making my second pot of coffee when the doorbell rang.

"Morning, Mr. Wainscot."

"Morning Sheriff."

He looked nonchalantly at the rifle barrel clutched in my right hand. "Going hunting?"

I leaned the gun up against the wall and left it there. "No. I was yesterday. Just cleaning it this morning."

"I see. Bag anything?"

I shook my head. "Nah. I'm a lousy shot. I just like to make the loud noises."

He laughed at that. "Happen to shoot any them dogs, maybe?"

"Not a one, sheriff, but I sure saw a few. Seemed an awful shame to me."

"Well, I'm just trying to get an idea on the count. See if we can get a handle on that pack. Apply some population control."

"Really?"

"Oh, yeah. They're a menace. You should know. You did Herb Dross's funeral, not five weeks ago. Last couple of years, they've gotten real aggressive too. Seem like they're coming for us like they've developed a taste, you know?" He was exaggerating for humor, but seemed to think the dogs were a menace that needed to be dealt with.

"That seems a little hard to believe."

"No, it's true. That's why I organized the hunt yesterday. That and I had a thought about Susie Dross. Passed my mind, maybe she'd been overcome and gone out to meet the same fate as her husband. You never know how grief is going to take hold of a body. I've seen stranger reactions. Anyway, it was worth a shot."

"I didn't know about it."

"I know. I didn't tell you. Never took you for the type, but Hal Upchurch said he saw you out there with your gun and everything..."

"Yeah, I saw old Hal. Scared the crap out of me."

"So. You're positive, you didn't shoot any dogs yesterday?"

"Never shot at any, anyhow."

"Alright then. Probably gonna have another hunt, next Saturday. Come on out, if you want."

* * *

It was a week that dragged along in slow motion. I held a suspicion that every breath I took would be my last. I didn't sleep either, just lay down for ritual's sake every night for an hour, then got back up for practicality. There was work to do and quickly. I just had to figure out what it was.

For reasons that didn't work themselves into my waking thoughts, I felt my own fate was tied to those dogs. We were scavengers all, picking the bones of the dead. The digestive system of this town. Should an asshole say, because I am not an eye, I do not belong to the body? Or likewise, the hands can not say to the stomach, we don't need you. But all the members of the body work together for the good of the body, and all the shit the dogs and I rolled in and spread around the town provided fertility to the soil of the population. We, the unseemly members, did we not deserve a greater honor and to be treated with special modesty? For if one member suffers, we all suffer. These were the particular strains of thought repeating in my head. My brothers were being hunted down, and when they were gone, I would be next.

There was rain for three days. It was cold and growing colder, but the rain at least softened the ground. People would notice fresh graves dug in the cemetery, so I had to take night trips out in to the country and find spots where I could plant a few. I knew enough to go deep. With the dogs around, I had to, to keep them from digging up the bodies. I'm not a young man now, sixty-three and the labor was taking its toll. Of course, at the cemetery I had machinery to do the digging, but out here, it was all me and the devil, and he helped out his fair share.

I gotta give him that.

Thanks to the cleaver and a chainsaw, I didn't

have to worry about lugging around anything shaped like a person. I economized on space and didn't fret over partials in a hole. If the right leg ended up in one spot and the left in another, it bothered me not at all.

Wednesday morning, I got a present. The Bojanski family of six were taken from us in an auto incident along with the driver of an eighteen-wheeler from out of town with enough amphetamine in his system to keep him walking hours after he'd passed. Sent the driver back home, but the Bojanskis were all mine. I made six fresh graves Friday, the night before the burial, using my digger and going down nine feet instead of the usual six. I packed away a dozen bodies, in pieces before filling the holes back in to the usual depth. Of course, I had to buy brand new caskets, one for each family member, though I did do some calculating and found some of the children small enough, that I could do the job with three. In the end, I decided the smart thing to do, was play it straight, as there would be plenty of attention focused on this service.

The Bojanskis provided the perfect excuse not to join the sheriff's hunting party Saturday. The service was in the morning and the burial immediately following. There were lots of friends and family from out of town in attendance. It was the largest ceremony I'd hosted in years.

In the distance, the pop of gunfire echoed and I flinched with every one. Several family members thanked me for the beautiful service and my heartfelt work, mistaking the origins of the emotion not concealed on my face.

Afterward I took the hearse and Winchester and went for a drive to the nearest spot the road would take me toward the dog hunt. I left the car and trudged off in to the woods to find the sheriff. They were not hard to find. I just walked toward the gunfire and figured I was getting close when I realized that I should be wearing one of those orange hunter's coats so I wouldn't get mistaken for anything else.

There was a sudden eruption of gunfire that didn't stop, but grew louder and more intense after a few seconds. It was a terrifying sound made of at least three different guns and joined by others from opposite directions after thirty seconds. There were yelps. The whole pack must've been caught in a low place. There was an incline straight ahead of me that I figured became a gulley on the other end, the rim of which the shooters must've been atop on the opposite side.

I kept walking toward it, and with trepidation began the ascent. From over the lip of the hill the sound of running feet came and I steeled myself. The first dog over the hill was a big beautiful animal with an ear missing, though that wasn't a recent wound. He was charging, leading the pack out of the trap, he'd led them into. The weight of leadership sat well upon his shoulders and propelled him down the hill toward me and I sank to my knees. If this was my time, I was ready to go. When he saw me, he altered his course some, but did not flag in speed and was followed by six more mutts running for their lives.

The last one over the hill, a short, wide wolfish looking creature yelped and tumbled over on his back and then back onto his front paws, but the back legs were done for. He'd caught a bullet with his hip and was going to die for it.

Didn't sit right with me.

I heard some shouts from up ahead and checked the action on the Winchester.

Hal Upchurch was the first one I saw. He came

into view on my right, in a run. He stopped and fit his rifle to his shoulder, aiming at the lead dog. I figured he didn't have a prayer of hitting his mark, but his intentions were enough to cause me to try my own impossible shot.

I was way off, but Hal took notice of me. He started waving his arms and yelling, figuring I hadn't seen him and was shooting at dogs still coming over the hill. I chambered the next round and let it go with a shout of my own. Hal ran away. So did I.

I raced back to the hearse, half hoping I wouldn't make it. I was tired and didn't particularly want to keep going. I was never going to get rid of the incriminating evidence in time. I'd clearly shot at Hal Upchurch, who would tell the sheriff soon enough and even if he wasn't quite believed, it'd warrant a home visit. Just seemed it would be easier if one of the dogs got me or the sheriff shot me in the back as I fled.

No dice. I made it to the car and even made it home. Inside, I dropped the rifle and ran to the kitchen. I put my head under the faucet on cold and took three slugs of Jameson. Then, for reasons I've never been able to satisfactorily explain, I went to the basement and grabbed the cleaver. I brought it up to the kitchen and placed my left hand, fingers spread, on the butcher block and took off the pinkie.

It was pretty impressive in retrospect. That's an odd angle and the chop was neat. I took the severed finger to the back door and threw it into the yard before collapsing in shock. They found me an hour later still holding my mangled hand and unresponsive, though my eyes were open.

* * *

Couple days later, I got a visit from Hunter Malcomson. Since we'd served on so many councils together, it seemed reasonable he might visit me at the hospital. The guard gave us the room. Hunter was pale and even though I promised that I had no intention of ever mentioning a thing about his involvement with me, he insisted on getting me a top lawyer. Whatever.

There's this program for prisoners to train puppies to be guide dogs. I've applied and been rejected three times, but maybe if I'm persistent, it'll happen. I understand they have to be careful who they recruit what with those PETA fuckers looking over their shoulders all the time. Gotta make sure I'm not gonna eat it. Or fuck it. Nothing could be further from my intentions and I should know. I keep telling them, I've got a pretty exhaustive self-knowledge.

Miriam

The first great mistake Miriam ever made, the one she'd been paying for the rest of her life was allowing herself ever to be born in the first place. By not succumbing to the sickness her mother passed on, she'd cavalierly thrown open the door for everything that came after. All the other missteps, bad decisions and sub-par moments really took their cue from that one. She reflected now and again how much you can owe for mistakes made in ignorance or even innocence, though the latter was not her experience.

Her mother lived in a Mississippi brothel near the Arkansas border another half year before she shot herself up with enough smack to kill a platoon and

MIRIAM

was buried, supposedly at midnight, under a tree overlooking the cat house, in an unmarked grave. The other girls had taken on the raising of Miriam as a hobby that helped keep their minds occupied when the life began to get to them and Miriam, still small and pink and given to fits of coughing and bouts of sleeplessness and without a trend toward feeding became a mascot of great importance to them.

Too young for intent, she became the confessional by virtue of helplessness and dependence. The ritual of rocking and cooing her over their shoulder whilst unburdening the day's trespasses into her tiny curved ear repeated nightly. She took in the very sweat and breath of sin and sighed and farted it back at them all cleaned up and smelling of infant. But it growed her up in an accelerated fashion such as was popularly believed by radio preachers to be the way in wicked times.

She learned things, as all children do, by osmosis and it colored the way she perceived the world and conducted herself in it. Though shy on use, she learned never to be in want of arms. She knew that cash was but one form of currency, that blessed by the Federal government which meant little much outside of legal documents. And she learned that sheep were wolves, sure as shit.

None among the rotating cast of mothers was more devoted to the child than the Nubian. She called the child Child and nourished her as one of the many she'd never birthed. Over time, she was generally acknowledged as the primary authority in matters concerning Miriam.

Her motherly ways were not demonstrated exclusive to the child and when Miriam was eleven, Auntie no shit Jemima got called upon to take over the madamship of a house in Hot Springs and brought her north. It was amidst the curious natural phenomena, claimed to purify a body and restore a soul, that Miriam first self administered opiates and then never looked back.

Auntie Jem knew the signs of junk better than your typical vice police and gave her a beating, like you reserve for the ones you love, the lines of which they are to read betwixt and comprehend the heighth and the breadth and the depth. Miriam was in bed afterward four days and reversed the cure just as soon as she walked. Jemima looked in the child's unfocused eyes, saw another sign she knew well, and changed up her tactic.

"If you make these vows, it will be more binding than any holy matrimony you aint never gonna enter into anyhow, an I oughtta know, so go on now an listen Auntie Jem." She taught the child heroin the way she'd taught her intercourse, as plain mechanical facts and proven strategies for recovery from. Flesh was one element among the bounty of creation and held unique properties like any other, but the real difference from wood and stone and sea and air and steel, was only possession.

"There now, then, that's everything I know. Jes don be letting it get in between you and what you need to do. An don ever let me catch you keepin mo secrets from me."

Tired of routine and itchy for the horizon the child ran off at age fourteen with a G.I. who'd seen Indochina. Among other promises, he claimed he would take her to exotic places and teach her worldly things. Two weeks later, her eyes open to nothing so much as the saming of America, she left him the clothes she'd used to tie him up with in a motel room off I-44 on the outskirts of Tulsa and took the rest of his belongings, including a photograph of his mother in a wide collared, floral print dress and high off the forehead construction of hair, as her own.

On her first night conscious of what alone in the world is meant to say, she removed the picture of the soldier's mother and spoke to it while sitting in a booth by the window of the Stuckeys. She thought she'd know what she wanted when she saw it and chances were, whatever it was could be found as likely in Tulsa as Toledo.

The picture, which she had not yet named, looked at her in a kindly but knowing way and a voice peculiarly like Jem's said "Child, you are alone."

"I know." she stated, without a value attached of emotional import.

"Where is it you going?"

Miriam shrugged.

"What is it you trying to leave behind?" Miriam spotted a bear of a man leaving the Stuckeys and ambling with a notion toward a sixteen wheeler parked on the far side of the lot. She slipped the picture back in her pocket and answered without listening.

"Only what I know."

* * *

MIRIAM

She worked the highway circuit and saw more of what she'd seen before. She carried a knife with a retractable blade, she'd only once had occasion to cut with. She'd used it on another drifter she'd spotted a curious amount at diners. Once, outside the Loaf 'N Jug, he surprised her by coming upon her while she slept. He had ideas he couldn't pay for and she reminded him of that by making him aware of the blade's tip in his kidney. His counter was to strike her face and she followed through by slicing deep and around to the front. It was enough to encourage him to roll off and she told him if she ever saw his mutt face again, she would certainly kill him.

Not all the familiars on the road were hostiles. Not to first impressions anyhow. She fell in with a boy she met doing a westerly drift originating from Bowling Green. He was nineteen, and thin as a reed with bear black hair, a bit long, and worn back with grease. His name was Casper and he met her by climbing into the cab belonging to a trucker who was distracted by the pickle tickle he was receiving from Miriam.

Casper, slick as duck shit, stepped in and placed his lady stinger behind the trucker's left ear. "Hoss, you got 'bout um ten more seconds to finish 'fore Ima need these here wheels." The trucker's boner did an immediate soft and Casper apologized. "Nah, Hoss, didn't mean for that to happen. Truly, I'm sorry. How much?"

The nervous trucker with his pants around his knees said "It's all in the glove box."

"Nah, I mean, how much you pay for the French?"

"Nothing."

"Nothing?" Casper looked Miriam in the eyes, "That so?"

Miriam wiped her mouth daintily, "He was going to drive me to California."

One second's consideration was all Casper needed. "No sweat, Hoss. I got it." He pulled the trucker, who was twice his size, out of the cab and hopped into the driver's seat. "I'll get her there, don't worry and I truly am sorry. Looked like your pleasure was sincere and I hate to disrupt that."

Miriam watched the trucker tug his jeans back up with both thumbs in the rearview, then fixed her eyes on Casper who glanced briefly in her direction, then focused on the road. He said, "Not enough sincerity these days. Not in people, don't you think?"

And she answered, "Are you for real?"

The way they worked it changed up. They targeted bowling alleys, veteran's halls and the occasional Y.M.C.A. Sometimes they'd be seen together and he'd be her brother and explain they needed money for traveling to their uncle's ranch after just losing their father to tragic circumstances. He would lean in and go on about how nice his sister was and how grateful she'd be for smiling on them in their need.

Other times, she'd arrive in the truck stop cafe alone, count out nickels enough for coffee and nurse it sallow cheeked, fishing for looks. Whatever the method, the climax was the same. Casper would slip in, apologize and leave with what he could carry. He gave the sincerity rap most times he made an entrance.

Then they would speed away, and with a fresh spike tapped, Miriam would sink into the deep enveloping grip of the leather seat and, with her feet, twist the dial of the A.M. radio. She'd switch back and forth between religious stations, just barely coming in, as though the open air were a winding, rut pocked trail sapping them the conviction to beg, once arrived. Casper, when her bare toes fell into his lap would change it back to rockabilly and tap the steering wheel unconsciously. Sometimes she raised her foot and punched an instrument of tuning only to be met by a single clear intonement coming out of the wilderness to "Repent. Make clear the way..." and Capser would nearly break the knob turning it off. He'd hum instead.

One such night, Miriam, trying to curl around the tickle making its way through her said, "Casper...you're what Auntie Jem would call a... hedonist."

"That so, Mirry? What is that, some kinda bible shit?"

"...guess so..."

"Sounds like bible talk." Then he rhapsodized about ancient things and the irrelevance of philosophy. Said weren't nothing thinking about preposterous hypotheticals could do for you now that you wouldn't do on your own without having wasted an hour and a minute, you could have been living, supposing. "Besides, all those bed sheet wearing pederasts never heard Gene Vincent." And with that, he drove the final nail into the coffin of rebuttal.

She liked the sound of that, far off sound that it was. It seemed to bounce around the car's interior something less than normal fast. It took banking paths off the windshield and dash into a slow cascading arc before reaching her ears. Other sounds were made that never did get there intact. They tended to arrive in fragmented syllables unlinked to any intentional meaning. Some said things escaped out the open windows when Casper would take a curve and she imagined them melting into the countryside to be picked up by wild beasts who knew no better than she what to do with them. But the timbre of his voice and reasoning appealed to her teenage sensibilities. She would volley something back occasionally mostly for the pleasure of provoking further ideological commentary. It was like listening to a conversation from underneath a bath.

* * *

"Tell me about your momma, Casper." She pulled out the G.I.'s wallet picture of his own mother, looking like an Eleanor or Gertrude or possibly a Helen. Her forehead was impossibly high and her mouth was small and dark and carried front teeth that met at an unlikely angle and which showed only a little bit between lips in her smile. Miriam was eager for traits to assign her imaginary matron, possessing, as she did, no picture of Auntie Jem.

Everything about the motel was thin. The walls were thin, the mattress was thin, the comforter was thin. Certainly the proprietor was thin, as was the smile meant to conceal his lechery when he handed Casper their room key. Casper'd paid extra this evening for a room with a television set and they'd decided to leave it on all night to get their money's worth.

Johnny Carson was sure a funny fella and made California seem like a nicer place than she already imagined. That was their stated destination and Casper meant to arrive on the top part and work their way down at a leisurely pace with an eye toward Mexico. He said they could make some money in California and it would spend better across the border.

Casper's lip curled reflexively. "My momma's a mean bitch, Mir."

Miriam turned over to face him, but he wasn't

looking her way. "No. You don't mean that."

"I'm sincere sugar. You gotta know least that."

"Why? What was so horrible about her?" Without thinking, she pressed the photograph to her breast as if protecting its ears from hearing the potentially hurtful things could be lobbed at a mother.

"Just mean. What else you want me to say?"

She didn't know. Anything would be better than mean, though. She'd seen enough of mean among the women of Jem's places. She'd seen other things too, but mean was a trait she'd grown weary of. It was a quality she was leaving out of photographic mother's personality. Betty, she decided she would name the picture, Betty. "Tell me if she could cook then."

"Course she could cook. Nothing to that. Not like fancy, but there's hardly a thing can't be choked down given the right treatments. Hell, anything that makes its own grease is got half the work done for you. So, yes, she didn't starve me. Thank you, momma."

She ignored the sarcasm in his voice and took the concession as a minor victory. Casper was a man of certainties, earned or not, and she was always pleased to discover a new area of gray in his views which she could continue to bring up until he'd pondered it thoroughly. He had no interest in discussing things he did not have a well formed or at least unretractable opinion on.

"Betty couldn't cook."

"Who?"

"My momma." She handed him the picture. "She didn't any ways. Auntie Jem did all that kind of work and Betty just made her hair pretty." She smiled at the ease the story came out with.

"Since I already got the pretty, I'm gonna learn to cook."

"Well, sugar now we know everything."

* * *

They had a pretty good thing going till she spoilt it by getting pregnant by him, or rather by telling him that she was. Her reluctance to say until she was most positive bought her only an uneasy spectator's type enjoyment of their time together. She watched those weeks like it was a T.V. show she'd like to be part of, knowing it was destined to end soon. When the sick was pretty much a constant, she said it. He shrugged the way was reflexive for him and gave her the options.

MIRIAM

"We been good together sweetheart and I will miss you if you go off and have this kid, but you wanna keep with me, don't worry none, the woods is full of sharp sticks." She spoilt it further by crying when she said she wanted to stay with him.

The next day he told her they could make a much better score by being more selective in their marks. They were somewhere near Lincoln when he explained what he meant. It was mid November and the sun wore out awful quick those days, so though it was not even five in the evening, dark had moved in and all but changed the locks on the doors when he stopped the Chevy across the street from a pool hall.

"Where is this?" She asked.

"Relax, Mir. I know this place. This is where we can make some good money." They crossed the street and he walked right through he puddles while she took care not to splash in them. He looked impatient with her, holding the front door open, waiting for her to catch up. The music warmed her instantly upon entering. Merle Haggard was having the same trouble with a lady he always seemed to be and it was a minor disappointment to realize that wouldn't change no matter where she went.

The warmth of the music in the air turned into a suffocating density of smoke emanating from a score of sources and holding everything in the atmosphere like a body of water. She could nearly see the disturbance sound waves made passing through, rippling out and disappearing in the corners of the broad hall. A dozen red felt tables in the front gave way to a bar that bisected the room. Casper led them between the tables; nodded at the man behind the bar and continued toward the back room where a short and round man with a cigar like a chicken leg clenched in his large teeth stood from his table and motioned Casper back.

She took a seat, as instructed on a high chair along the wall and watched Casper go toward the fat man. He talked to the proprietor and she saw him give the man some money. The barman brought her a vanilla Coke while Casper spoke about business in the back.

When he returned to her side, he had a root beer bottle featuring a straw sticking out the top. "Who is that man?" she inquired, watching him with his back to them now, speaking into a telephone mounted on the wall.

MIRIAM

Casper didn't look at her, but kept his eyes on the customers going about their games and drinks. Most of the patrons looked like farmers to her, though she couldn't reconcile what seemed like the hardest work in the world with recreation of this sort, in her thinking. They wore overalls, anyhow. There were teenagers at the front tables. Tall, angular sticks of boy men, the fattest part of them, impossibly large Adam's apples protruding from throats that had never been shaved. Five Negro men, dressed like whites in overalls and denim caps, shared a table nearest to the bar. They had given her some consideration, but looking at Casper, knew better than to waste their time making advances.

"Fat man." he answered like it meant something.

"What does that mean?"

"Means he's fat, Mir. Don't worry now. He's gonna hook us up with deep pockets." Over the next two hours, Casper had turned down a couple of dudes who eventually approached them, getting a head shake from the fat man. When a respectable looking one about fifty entered and caught Casper's eye, he triangulated the gaze with the manager who nodded. Casper sucked the rest of his cream soda through the straw and said, "Bingo. Be right back."

He made his way across the room to the man, in the expensive clothes. They conversed briefly, both throwing over the shoulder looks back and bargaining for her. An agreement was reached and Miriam was approached by the man who failed to hide his reptilian nature underneath his expensive clothes and refined manner. Miriam knew the drill, but still felt a shiver getting the go ahead from Casper through the smoke.

He was all of a gentleman meeting her. Called her miss and held out his arm for her to join in the walk out the hall. He had a big black hearse of a car waiting which made her nervous some. Meant Casper would have a driver at least to dispatch of before he could make an entrance, but her love for and trust in Casper had yet to be proved unfounded.

Her concern increased when instead of taking her to some flea bag motel or fuck pad bungalow, he took her to a proper home in a respectable neighborhood and pulled right in to the driveway bold as innocence. She'd heard of such places before, but had to call this a first actually being there. On the television programs she'd seen, these streets seemed common and were home to the best people society had produced and she'd appropriately taken the underlying message speaking at her through television console in the back room at Jem's place to be that this was not where she belonged.

The driver, a big soft Negro with a shiny head and white smile, he wasn't using, opened her door and helped her out. The gentleman had already entered the home and the African instructed her toward a secondary structure round the back of the main house.

"Go on now, make yourself comfortable and whatever you do-" He inclined his head in a conspiratorial manner, "-don't speak to him and don't look him in the eye."

Walking toward the guest house, she tossed a look over her shoulder trying to find Casper's Chevy. Even as she entered, she felt the ink drying on that chapter of her life. She paused internally to consider what was to be learned and what could be taken with her into the next. There were things she knew would not pass through the fire, but she wasn't certain what they might be.

By the next morning it was apparent that Casper

had deserted, sold her and their baby to the well groomed monster. She never spoke to another soul about her ordeal that night with the amateur abortionist, but she saw him in her sleep for years, standing over her strapped to a table, reciting from memory, passages of medical texts, poetry and all manner of school learned appreciations while he experimented. She exercised a tight grip on her voice and refused to cry out and send any extra pleasure toward him, though she was dehydrated from the tears flushed silently throughout.

She was abandoned in the woods fifteen miles outside the city with some water and a towel for the bleeding. She was too weak to walk the first day. The void where the fetus had been throbbed, keeping her from sleep. Over the course of the day, though she could not put words to the process, it filled with something darker and harder and colder by far than she'd ever guessed at in her nature. In the dusk that eventually fell, she heard dogs circling her, attracted to the blood in the air, but she passed the night unmolested.

One and counting.

*　*　*

MIRIAM

Aunty Jem never betrayed the flip flop her heart did when she saw Miriam again. The child showed up at the doorstep as the last customers of the previous night were making their departures. Miriam was looking like just another starlet deciding to face facts. Aunt Jay's saw them occasionally; the ones that got out of California before dying poorly nearer to the farm they grew up on. She had the costume, but not the posture of that particular breed of prodigal.

Her clothing was gray and frayed and the marks about her where skin showed told stories she'd been warned against. Her face featured dark places beneath her eyes and her teeth looked less white than they had the last time she was seen, but there was never any mistaking her. Jem saw her coming a hundred yards down the road.

"Child." said Jem in her deep, rich voice. It felt to Miriam like hot butter sliding over her face and she imagined it filling in the many cracks and depressions she'd added in her sojourn. She carried everything she could call her own in a single over the shoulder bag, the approximate size and weight of a house cat. The essentials she carried on her person always. Her knife in the top of her boot, any pills or powders she had left in the toe of the opposite and cash concealed in various private spots.

"Hey Jem."

"How long you staying?"

"Just long enough."

"I see. Well come in and get out those rags. I'll have Sugar fetch you something clean."

Betty had talked her through the woods and found them a Salvation Army. She'd told the case worker then about hitchhiking to her momma's home in Portland. Said she'd miscarried and been left in the woods by a spooked driver. She'd let the woman read whatever she wanted into that. They'd fixed her up with a couple nights' sleep and food as would keep you from starving.

She relayed the same story to Jem, minus the bunk about family while she cut Miriam's hair after a hot bath and afternoon nap. "I'm ready to pull my own weight around here, Jem."

"Says you."

"Taught me good."

"You all gristle and bone, child. Rest up some."

"I'm not around for long, Jem. You know that?"

"Spect as much. Don go till you ready, though."

MIRIAM

Miriam did not cry in front of Auntie Jem, but rather waited for the time when she was alone in Jem's bed, to curl up like a baby and let loose some of the hurt and fear she'd kept strapped to her. She gave voice to some of the bitter parts, followed by hushed admissions of scares she'd acquired since leaving home. She'd made them audible, which was as far as it would go. She'd let them out that far, but kept a tight leash on them and kept them close and they licked at her body like hungry puppies until sleep was a fact requiring no acknowledgment or cooperation.

Jem stayed on the other side of the door, joining the child in a tear letting and came in to stroke her hair when she fell to sleep. Miriam slept without dreams for a single merciful night.

She'd asked Jem to style her hair up off of her forehead, but never disclosed where the notion came from; suspecting Jem would worry more than she ought when Miriam took her leave again. The result was something of a disappointment to her, but as she negotiated with the mirror she made something more like agreeable terms when she employed heating instruments.

She found work in the house and yard to occupy her body while her mind resolved whatever it was working around. She learned something about cooking too. As she put on weight, Jem encouraged her toward town, saying there was plenty opportunity for a woman not afraid to work and she could do her proud by carving out a respectable life, independent of the needs of men. She always rebuffed Jem's suggestions by informing her that she had needs of her own that didn't fit any cozy, over the fire place type pictures and leave it at that.

Her needs were not yet in focus, but called to her louder all the time.

One morning, Miriam slipped out while Jem made up the room. This surprised neither. She returned to the highway, plying her trade for distance and sustenance, heading once again for California, because that was where the road ended.

* * *

The man behind the bar just wanted to wash his glasses and not give the time of day to the young girl with the short styled haircut and attitude. He'd had her pegged as soon as she'd come in. Sex fell off her like breath and as much as he might like a ride, he knew when he was over his head. So he only attempted to answer her question. "Where you headed?"

Miriam leaned in to savor the sulfur smell of the struck match as testament to the general fragrance of the honky-tonk. When the scent died, she would rely on the cigarette.

"Casper."

"Wyoming?"

Miriam looked the bartender in the eyes. "You know any other?"

"Guess I just never met nobody headed to. Coming from, sure, but headed to? On purpose? Don't come across that much round here."

"Got some kinda high opinion of this place, huh?"

"You don't?"

"Nothin special, far as I can see. Who is it I should meet?"

He indicated a cluster of bearded men hovering over a pool table, great swollen guts hanging over the front of their pants, all covered in once white t-shirts that ran the length and the width and the return trip underneath back to the jeans they tucked into.

Suspenders and ball caps rounded out the club uniform. She'd spotted them the moment she'd entered. Knew the look, knew the type. "Anybody particular?"

The bar tender shrugged. He suggested something along the lines of "Bitch." under his breath as she slid off her stool and wiggled her narrow ass at him across the room.

"Who's the fortunate gentleman going to make my acquaintance on the way to Casper this evening?" she offered by way of introduction. This turned heads in the general direction of her feet and she waited patiently, posing while they slowly turned northward.

One of the younger stood up and squared his shoulders, centering his fleshy hands on his cue. He tilted his red cap back on his head and offered "Missoula?"

She took a pouty puff on her cigarette. "Don't even rhyme, now do it?"

* * *

She found she needed neither his presence nor advice to have success as was equal to what they'd had as a team. She certainly didn't need his blathering mouth, certain of its own importance and just about full of shit. She also felt no great loss when considering his affections, seeing in a behind her now way how hollow a gesture they had been.

If there were two ways of learning a thing, Miriam would always choose the bloody. This scholarly style had a way of marking her so that every year showed. At seventeen, she made another near fatal mistake. Having set out for California, she'd ricocheted off the coast line and found herself touring Wyoming. She was making a concentrated effort to escape the orbit of the region and spotted a likely ticket elsewhere at the cash register. He was headed south by southeast and she said good enough. Her appetite for wandering not yet replaced by anything else, Miriam continued to work in trucks and that night she hesitated to pull her weapon at the first itch to. The result was she got a detached retina from making the acquaintance of the dashboard with his hand behind her head forcing the meeting to take place rapidly and without time to prepare.

The further result was she took another beating, like perhaps the kind you would like to give a loved one except they aren't there and you wish they were and would read between the lines, understand exactly what you meant. She's not all the way conscious for most of it.

The beating was received after she took off the tip of his pecker with her front teeth when she woke up in a dark place. She felt like her insides were jelly. Sore jelly like a great, single bruise. The pungent smell in the enclosed space was familiar as was the difficulty walking. She had to shut her damaged eye to make sense of the place, such as was available to be made.

She spotted her assailant asleep, without his trousers, on a cot ten feet and as many painful shuffles away. Apparently there'd been a party. He'd had red rimmed eyes and favored her with darty amphetamine glances when he'd first picked her up, and it looked like he'd spent up a year's worth of twitch while he drove. Judging from the all smashed together feeling her guts were reporting, his fornication style was jackhammer and goodnight.

He looked now like every man she'd ever met and had no detail to him at all. In the other direction was escape out the door of his truck, she reckoned herself rightly to be in the back of. The consideration of options lasted not half a minute. She went about it slow and with great care, not wanting to spoil the opportunity presented her. Carefully, she motioned herself, with great pain, till she was kneeling over him. She found it hidden within itself like a woodland creature sheltering in the roots of a tree and used her fingers gently to coax it out. It responded to her mouth and once she had its confidence she bit down.

The grip she employed was not one designed to preamble escape, but held rather a weight that lent legitimacy to the permanence of her claim. It belonged to her now, the way she'd seen terrier dogs lay hold of a toy. She'd seen them lifted off the ground, supported only by their stubborn grip. She knew that there was finality in those clinched jaws.

When he separated her from him, she retained possession of his dickhead and smiled away as he lay into her with his hands. Eventually he passed out and she was not killed that day, though she told herself she was prepared to die. She would be his last victim and decided that it was also her last time to be one. There was a leverage of power in the ability to follow through your intentions with the possibility of death introduced. She felt it for the first time that night, his flesh now hers swallowed and not to return. Let him do what he needed, she'd only done the same.

In the end, she did it because revenge was holding sway over her hierarchy of needs. She'd got away before, but had never taken revenge. It tasted sweet. Revenge, not his pecker.

She woke again near the back of the rig, gray light insisting its way between the floor and swinging doors. There were still stars visible in the pre dawn sky and the cold air ran toward invigorating, though she was not a candidate for walking. She strained her neck toward the draft and breathed what she could of freedom. It was enough.

She felt unconsciousness taking her again, but did not fight. She was ready for whatever came next, on the first page of a new chapter in her life.

One and counting.

The Morning After

Saturday

Terry rooted through the pantry for kibble, but there wasn't any. Beth hated the dog as an extension of him and she never bought it any food. He'd brought the puppy home the day before she came back from the hospital with their first born. He figured it was only fair.

One for him, one for her.

Six months later, she'd given him the weekend to get his things out while she took the baby to visit her mother in Fayetteville. Layla whined and turned in circles as he pushed aside cans of corn and peas, green beans and Gerber bananas.

He'd collected his clothes from the front lawn and found her note nailed to the front door. Be gone by Monday. His stuff, con- sisting primarily of baseball cards, pocket knives and 8mm stag films, was pretty well picked over by the time he'd come home that afternoon and what was left had been damaged by the morn- ing's rain. He recovered a print or two that had sheltered under his clothes. Three Orifices of Eve and Bush-War had either been unpopular or undiscovered and would have to suffice for a while.

Ronald and Tink Hodge, the neighborhood moron twins, had a habit of going through houses during work hours and had absconded with the lion's share of his things. The twelve year olds had pilfered his stash before and he'd made no fuss. He figured he was a lot of things, but not a hypocrite. Beth had complained for months about his disinterest in protecting their home and then she had a shit fit when he bought the puppy.

The fuck did she think it was for anyway?

He grabbed the pistol from the closet and his Styx records, left the lava lamp and black light posters. Everything he grabbed would fit in the cab of his pickup. Then he'd got his easy chair lodged in the front door, unable or unwilling to maneuver it any further by himself. Now the dog was going apeshit for kibble and it was ten minutes past Miller time. So he settled on a personal favorite.

"Ready for a treat?" he asked the dog. The whir of the can opener sent her into hysterics until the click of her nails on the linoleum sounded like Gregory Hines on speed. Spaghetti-O's always gave her diarrhea, but that wasn't his problem any more. He set the bowl down in front of her and grabbed a longneck from the fridge.

In the front room he collapsed into his chair at an awkward angle, suspended some ten inches off the floor and it gave a couple back. He wrapped his lips around the beer and set to contemplating whether or not it was the sorriest day of his life. Had he misjudged his wife's moral fiber and pushed her too hard or simply never cared about their union and prepared from the beginning for this inevitable outcome?

The chair creaked, then crashed onto the porch under his weight, leaving gashes in the door frame and tears in the vinyl, but he was out, officially and for good. Layla came scampering in to inves- tigate the sound and leaped into his lap. She sniffed at his crotch and then his face and burped. A Chef-Boi-Ardee and dry cereal cloud hung level with his head. He fanned at it with his right hand.

"Good shit, huh?"

* * *

The Gulch was as dark as you'd ever want it to be even at three in the afternoon. Day and night passed unnoticed since there were no clocks or windows and the low-watt lighting above the bar acted as a beacon for those that could still walk, to make their way toward the goods, but it did not illuminate any of the surrounding area, a fact for which the Gulch's patrons were grateful. "Hoah, lookie whose mommy let him out to play." The greeting was too loud and woke up a pair of regulars dozing in the corners. Terry tipped his imaginary hat to Cal Dotson sitting at the bar and sidled up beside him. Cal wrinkled his nose. "Judas priest, you smell like Saigon snatch on Monday morning."

"Don't get any ideas, pervert. Buy me a drink."

Cal threw a peace sign at the bartender and said "Hey, man, two." He turned toward Terry and looked him over. "Aren't you afraid you'll catch a scolding?"

Terry grabbed his Bud and finished it without coming up for air. He shook his head. "I am single and all a-tingle."

"No shit?"

"None. Beth kicked my ass to the curb. I'm moved into my dad's old place." He dropped his wedding band into the community jar where it clinked against the many that had taken up permanent residence there. It was worth a free pitcher.

Cal clapped him hard on the back. "Congratu-fuckin-lations. Let's celebrate."

"I am broke, like flat."

"S'okay. We'll drive out to Springfield and make a withdrawal from 7-11, then pick up some honeys at the Salvation Army. Get your tootsie rolled."

They took Terry's truck and made their way along 71 toward Springfield. Terry chose a spot he'd not hit before and coasted around the back of the convenience store. It was the main attraction of a mini strip mall also home to a beauty supply and a pawnshop, neither of which looked to be doing business. Cal made fat lines of speed on the dash and cut into a Hardees straw, giving half to his partner.

They burst through the front door with grocery bags over their heads, unable to see clearly unless they used one hand to hold the eyeholes gouged in their plastic masks flush to their faces. To compensate for limited vision, they turned their torsos continually in severe arcs with pistols drawn to cover the whole store.

"What's good here?" shouted Cal as he grabbed the lone clerk by his shirt and planted the barrel of his gun under the young man's chin. "Down on your fuckin' knees, now." Terry covered the store, rounding up a heavy set woman with a teenage daughter in tow and a swell-gutted man of about thirty with a camouflage ball cap on his dome.

"You, you and you, over there." He instructed them to the back corner of the store nearest the restrooms and the office. The three trudged backward with their hands up 'till they were against the wall. Terry turned his head slightly and yelled for his partner. "Clear."

Cal hopped over the counter and instructed the clerk to empty the cash drawer while he scanned the shelves for high-end swag. The heavy woman was trying to hide her cut-off wearing, poky-tittied, piece of jailbait daughter from Terry.

"What's on that t-shirt?" He asked. The girl stepped around her mother. She sported bangs highover her forehead and braces gleaming off her teeth. On her face, her natural irritation with old people was losing a battle against fascination with his disregard of the law and snub-nosed phallus cradled confidently in his hand. The t-shirt in question was for the Silver Bullet Band and she let him read it rather than say. "You like Seeger, Lil' Bits?" She nodded, defying him to say something evil about her tastes. "Yeah, he's not bad, I guess. I thought it was Floyd at first, though. You like Floyd?"

She shrugged.

"That's right, you're a little young for them. How old are you anyway?"

"Fourteen and a half."

Fourteen. Sweet mother, he felt old. "You get your period yet?" She blushed and got back to the shady side of her momma, who spoke through clinched teeth to Terry.

"You say one more thing to her, asshole and I'll

rip your dick off and roast it on a spit."

"Yeah, okay. You do that now."

"Hoah, man, lookiddit. Videos." Terry turned around and fol- lowed Cal's pointing finger across the store toward the video section. "Awwright."

Finished clearing the register, Cal grabbed another sack for videocassettes and started scooping the shelves clean into the bag. He enlisted the clerk's help with the task. "Hey man" Cal nudged him with his pistol from behind, "you got a nudie section?"

"Uh-uh."

"How 'bout one of those machines? You rent machines?" The clerk nodded his head. "Well let's have one of them too." The clerk came out from behind the counter carrying a V.C.R. the size and shape of a small suitcase. "Awesome. Give it to my partner."

Terry took the machine by its handle. He guessed it weighed thirty pounds. He watched the customers and they watched Cal and the clerk gather videocassettes into plastic bags. Each one held roughly the contents of a single shelf and as soon as it was filled, it was placed on the floor with the others. Then Cal or the clerk would run back to the counter for another sack. After three trips, Cal just brought a bunch of bags back to the video section with him. Pleased with himself for this innovation, he stood back and let the clerk bag the rest.

The sheer volume of their haul threatened to overwhelm his pickup, but infused with crank confidence, and with his eyes bulg- ing, Terry vowed to watch every one of the tapes they took.

When they were finished, Terry locked the clerk and the cus- tomers in the manager's office and cut the phone line. The plastic bags were bulging and spilling their contents in the parking lot. He and Cal each took four and left more behind as they ran out the front door. The sight of so many movie cassettes made them giddy and they laughed all the way to Springfield.

"Hoah, shit. Next time we'll have to hit a spot with a porno section. I can't believe I never thought of it."

"Swear to me, man, we're gonna watch every one."

"What'd we get? Tell me you got the bag with Firewalker." They found a cheap room and paid for two days, then hid their haul inside before seeking company.

They pulled in to the lot that the Salvation Army shared with the thrift store and the grocery. Pockets bulging with quarters destined for the Shop 4 Less' arcade, they walked into the sunlight and strode coolly past the Army's offices, scanning the front win- dows for potential party girls. They ambled on toward the thrift store and the pop machine on the corner. Shastas uncorked, the delicious sound of the fizzy drinks mirrored their insides perfectly and as mating calls go, there are less effective ones used in the summer heat.

Sunday

The crank had soured in their guts five hours earlier and their teen- age dates had split ten minutes later. As orgies go, it hadn't been much. Cal and the skinny blond had kept to themselves leaving her chubby friend alone with Terry. She had no technique, but was mercifully unselfconscious and up for whatever.

Cal kept feeding tapes into the machine, each time eliciting giggles from the girls. The four of them had watched six movies in one night. There were strong feelings for both Ghoulies and Police Academy expressed between the quartet, but nothing matched the response to American Ninja, hands down, the hit of the evening.

Cal said he was going to get himself a tape machine soon and the skinny blond said she'd had one all to herself back when she'd lived with her parents. "No way." Said Cal. "Why'd you ever run away then?"

"My dad kinda freaked out when he caught me blowing his best friend."

"Nuh-uh."

"Yeah, things were a little too weird around the house after that." Terry turned that scenario over in his head for hours after they'd left.

Cal wasn't puking anything up anymore, just flexing his throat muscles and making noise. "Use some aerosol, please, man." Cal went on wretching. Terry tossed a can at the toilet from across the room.

"This is hairspray, asshole."

"Like I care. Use it."

"Being married sure made your smell holes delicate." Calwalked back to his twin bed and Terry tossed him a 12 oz. apol- ogy. He settled in and wiped his mouth with the bed sheet. "What's this one called again?"

"H.O.T.S."

"Is it just me, or isn't that the little dude from Brady Bunch?" On screen there were two sororities who had issues between them, settling accounts with a game of strip-football. It was a pretty decent contest. "Shit. You got a kid now, too, huh?"

"Uh-huh."

"Fucks you up a bit, I bet." Terry'd had to rip a plastic shield off the back of the motel's T.V. to hook up the video machine and he was leaning toward leaving the damn thing attached when they checked out. He was getting sick of movies.

"Yeah. Looks like me even."

Cal was unconscious.

Tuesday

Terry and Cal braced each other for the stroll from his truck to the front door of his dead father's house. The grocery bag of cash was near empty and Beth had left his dog tethered to the front porch.

Layla was cheering them on like a coach at the Special Olympics. Terry reached her first and had six layers of sweat replaced on his face by extra strength dog gob. The puppy's tongue flicked excitedly and tickled the roof of his mouth and back of his teeth.

He was happy he'd traded one bitch for the other.

Thursday

The sound of the front porch creaking woke him up and he gripped the snub-nose underneath the couch cushion. There was no knock. Beth came in carrying little Wendell who was dressed only in a suspicious looking diaper. His hair was already too long and his nose was runny, though he didn't look like he'd been crying.

"Had the locks changed, Terry. Had to. Just wanted you to know, your key won't work anymore. You got your truck and your chair and your dog. Anything else you want, you're gonna have to break a window. Here." She handed the infant to him and went to inspect the contents of his refrigerator. "Judas priest, Terry. What are you going to feed Wendell?" I sure as hell don't see anything here. I'd have brought some canned Italian, only some asshole fed it all to the dog. Plus all the Cheerios. Which then got shit-sprayed all over my rug."

Terry smiled involuntarily, but caught himself when he felt tiny fingers grab his nose. He looked into his son's face and instantly recognized himself. Freaked him out. He put Wendell on the floor and tried to stand up with some authority. "What are you doing in my house?"

Beth faced him with her fists resting on her hips. "I have still got a job. I didn't spend the first half of the week sleeping off the weekend. Mrs. Edwards can't take him today, so you've got to. The plant called and fired you official yesterday, so I knew you'd be available." She walked past him and picked up their baby. She kissed Wendell fiercely and set him back on the floor. On her way out the door she said, "I'll be back by six."

Layla was sniffing at the baby and then they were both look- ing up at him.

1998 Was a Bad Year

It was his turn with the kid this week. Beth was out of town with some new boyfriend who was taking her all manner of places she'd always whined about wanting to visit. Good luck, bro, thought Terry. See if she lets you in the back door now. Since Wendell was with him and he had to work hard to score points in the dad department, Terry'd decided to teach the boy to drive.

Wendell was thirteen and it was embarrassing how soft he was. That was his mother's fault. She was always spoiling him, always cuddling him as a baby when he cried. Maybe that shit worked with girls, but you had to be tough on boys. It's a cruel thing to not whip boys, they've gotta learn about things young so that they can handle it when the world takes off its belt.

A bonus to having the squirt around and knowing how to drive was that Terry could get stinko at the Gulch without chancing another DWI on the way home. He pinned a note to his jacket instructing the bartender, who would find him passed out or incapacitated, to get the kid out of the Monte Carlo on the corner to help him out the door.

It must have worked because when the banging in his head woke him up he was on his own bed. His jeans were wet and cold about the crotch, but the bedding looked to have been spared the worst of it. The banging started again and sent regret throbbing through his head. He heard someone talking in the other room followed by the creak of the front door. "Who was that?" he called to Wendell.

"Run, Dad! It's the police!" Came the immediate reply. Like a hungover robot, Terry's legs shot out from under him and carried him toward the bedroom door. He tipped over his dresser to block the way, then slid the window open and jumped through kicking his legs spasmodically and landed upon his head in the lumpy lawn outside his bedroom. As soon as he hit the ground, he rolled into a crouch and sprinted through the back yard into the woods, over the creek and north toward St. Louis.

After five minutes of flat out running, which had slowed to a sloth's pace, he fell to his knees and puked a puddle of yellow liquid that would surely kill the grass. Then he rolled over and passed out.

He woke again to banging in his head. It felt like someone was trying to jackhammer their way out from behind his eyeballs. When he got to his feet and began the long trek to civilization, he tried to remember why he'd slept in the woods. He'd heard Wendell say 'run' and 'police', and instinct had carried him to that spot, but he might've overreacted.

When he found that he was on autopilot, heading for the Gulch, he smiled. Good old autopilot. He was there before the jackhammer guy seemed close to getting out and Terry tried to tickle him to passivity with a hair of the dog.

Cal Dotson came in after a half hour and called out when he saw Terry. "Hoah, the man of the hour." He beamed like Terry'd just made him a grandfather as he crossed the dark void between them and sat on the adjoining stool. Cal clapped Terry hard on the shoulder and then smacked the bar with equal enthusiasm. "Bartender, do not accept a

1dime from my friend here. Everything he wants tonight is on me. In fact-- " Cal looked around and counted the patrons up to two, "--next round is on me."

The bartender grunted and the other two drinkers said, "Fuck you" in unison. The drinks were poured and didn't have to wait long to be picked up. Cal smiled at each of his benefactees and ignored their sour expressions while he explained the reason they were celebrating.

"My friend here is a published author as of three days ago." Nobody cared, but Cal continued. "And like all great authors, he confronts the establishment in his time and lives in mortal danger of its wrath, all the while sowing seeds of immortality in the hearts and minds of all those who read his words." He drained his Bud and signaled for another before the empty glass was on the bar. "His ideas, once released, can never be called back or quieted. They sally forth and do not return void."

The bartender poured himself a drink too,

slammed it, and then said. "The fuck you going on about?"

Cal made as if he were sizing up the bartender and the clientele, then placed his hand upon Terry's shoulder. "You look, to me, like gentlemen of the world and as such it may warm your hearts to hear that Terry here fucked the sheriff's daughter." Indeed, there was a mumbled appreciation of this claim.

"And furthermore, my colleagues of discriminating taste, he chronicled the event." Terry felt his balls tingle, as Cal's story was just now cutting through the alcoholic fog that gripped his mind. "Then he published the story in High Society magazine."

The bartender raised his eyebrows.

"It's electric out there." Cal gestured toward the outside world. "Everybody's talking about it. Blaylock's is sold out and they're disappearing from all the liquor stores in a fifty mile radius. You my friend, my hero, must take precaution. Please finish your refreshments and then go underground. Follow the drinking gourd and trust no one till they talk funny."

Ah, thought Terry. Now it makes sense. He began to giggle uncontrollably. The thought of Sheriff Mondale finding the published account of his wild kid's kinky habits in the hands of every deadbeat loser in town made him happy. Cal joined him and after an interval, even the bartender smiled and poured another round.

After a few minutes, the wisdom of Cal's advice also crept in. The police had already been to his house. They were probably looking for him now. Mondale was going to nail his ass. He needed to create some distance between himself and Johnny law. Suddenly panicked, he turned to Cal. "You got any cash for me?"

Cal shook his head. "But such as I have I give unto thee." He took a set of keys out of his pocket and placed them on the bar. Take care of her, amigo and bring her back soon, but go now. Be smart."

Terry slapped the keys off the bar and clapped his friend on the back. Cal was right. He hadn't thought this through that well. He really should take off for a spell. Wendell would be fine on his own for a few days. Probably have the time of his life, maybe even ditch his virginity.

1998 WAS A BAD YEAR

He found Cal's pickup outside and stepped into the cab. He was dimly aware of eyes on him – the famous outlaw who'd defiled the sheriff's little girl. He was still woozy and decided to skip taking a bow. The engine started right up and he was shifting into reverse when he heard the hood smashed. Startled, he looked into the cold dead eyes of justice.

Sheriff Mondale's fist left a ham-sized dent in Cal's truck. Terry looked around and saw that they, indeed, had an audience. The Gulch emptied as well as the grocery on the corner. The clerks had abandoned their posts and stood with their faces smashed against the glass storefront to see him die. Traffic stopped going both directions and the whole thing played half speed.

Cal stood there, in the doorway, guiltily nursing his beer while his best friend was about to die. The sheriff walked around the front of the truck while Terry sat still and dumb. When Mondale got to the door, Terry pushed the lock down. Mondale reached in the open window and pulled up on the mechanism. Terry slapped it back down and started rolling up the window. Mondale just pulled the glass completely out and it shattered on the pavement.

The sheriff didn't bother opening the door. He reached for Terry, who slapped ineffectually at the giant hands, and hauled his redneck ass through the window. Mondale's grasp swallowed up Terry and held him by both hands, then by both wrists.

He slid Terry's left hand under his right arm so that he could hold Terry's right hand in both of his own. Terry started screaming a hysterical, high-pitched scream. "Please, no. No, no, no, no. I didn't know, I swear." His fingers wriggled and writhed, but eventually were subdued. When his middle finger was secured, Terry took a deep breath.

The snap stopped time.

His finger made an unnatural 'L' with the other then dangled backward like a wet noodle. The breath leaked out of him and he sucked pathetically for more, but didn't find any. The process was repeated with far less struggling on his left side.

Everything hurt. He was helpless like a fuckin' mental cripple. Both middle fingers broken near off, were taped to the ring fingers. Everything was hard to do: eating, dressing, bathing, driving. Forget about work, he couldn't handle a riding lawn mower, let alone a CAT, which left him many idle hours. And that was even worse. He couldn't shuffle cards or tug his meat and daytime TV was for housewives. Hell.

He called Beth, which was an accomplishment in itself and asked if she wouldn't mind letting the kid stay with him more while he was incapacitated. She agreed right away, which made him feel worse. That meant she was probably still getting some from that new guy. There was no satisfaction in getting what he wanted if it didn't involve depriving someone else of theirs. But Wendell would be helpful to have around. He'd do just about anything Terry asked, then retreat to a corner to remain unnoticed until needed again. If only his mom had been that way.

Thursday night, Cal picked him up at six and Terry told Wendell not to expect him back all weekend. His son took the news stoically and Terry wondered if the kid's delicate feelings were hurt or if he was stoked to have the place to himself. Sadly, it was probably the former. He was a strange kid. When Terry was that age, he'd have given his left nut for run of the house for a weekend. Oh well.

Cal was happy. Thursday was usually the best part of the weekend, and he regularly called out sick or just didn't go in to work on Fridays. They headed for the Gulch and hit happy hour in the face. Each of them ordered a pitcher of Bud and three shots of Tequila. Terry shared his painkillers and the weekend had begun.

Two hours later, the cocktail of motor skill assassins had rendered Terry clumsy and he spilled the last of his second pitcher and cussed. "At this rate, I'll be dry by Sunday."

"Won't let it happen, kemosabe." Cal laughed. He grabbed his own pitcher and took it over to the next table. Charlie and Toby, the men already sitting there weren't happy to see him.

"Fuck off," the older one said as soon as Cal had settled and begun to pour himself another drink. Cal ignored him and drained half the glass in a single gulp. "Hey. Did you hear me? Fuck off, like now."

"Get bent, Charlie."

"What did you say?"

"Go out back and play with each other quietly, so the rest of us can finish a

drink," said Cal. Toby, the younger one, stood up and Cal kicked his knee from under the table with a steel toe. The young man fell and smacked his face on the edge of the table, sending all the drinks and glass that rested atop crashing to the floor. "Son of a bitch!" cried Cal, seeing his unfinished pitcher go to waste. He reached across the table and smashed his mug on the side of Charlie's head.

Quickly as he could, Terry made his way over and began kicking Toby in the ribs. If Toby managed to get to his feet, Terry would be useless with his mangled hands, but it didn't happen. Terry connected the heel of his cowboy boot to Toby's temple and the youngster stopped moving.

A horse kicked Terry in the kidneys and he collapsed with a whimper. The bartender stood over him with a well used baseball bat. "Get the fuck out, now!" Cal and Charlie stopped their 'rasslin and together dragged Toby's unconscious body out the back door while Terry followed, unable to contribute because of his hands.

When they'd propped Toby up against some garbage bags, Terry made his contribution by taking out the last of his painkillers which all three of them split. Charlie dry-swallowed his, then looked down at the man on the ground. "Shit. There goes my ride."

"You can ride with us." said Cal.

"You are a white man," said Charlie, "and I

know a place."

"Oh yeah? Like a reasonable place? How much?" Charlie reached into his back pocket and took out his Saturday Night Special.

"We can make a stop first."

"Okey-doke."

The Mexican population was a small, but growing minority in town, a fact that alarmed most of the citizens. They were a cluster that were rarely spotted outside the borders of Beantown, but were large enough to have their own grocery store that stocked mini tortillas and a rainbow coalition of salsa and beans. They also had their own video store with Mex titles starring big-tittied, big-hipped Mex starlets, and that were big on guns and mustache wax. They also had their own liquor store.

The volume wouldn't be large enough to make a worthwhile score of the cash register, but there was a neighborhood Mex lottery held on Friday nights and Charlie figured they could hit that stash tonight for enough to make a good weekend for the three of them at a brothel he knew in West Memphis.

One advantage, Charlie figured, was that it probably wouldn't even be reported to the police, seeing as how the lottery was unregulated. "Rock on," agreed Cal and Terry opened the window so that the breeze would brace him enough to be a getaway driver.

They parked across the street and Cal put the car in neutral and pulled the parking brake. Terry slid beneath the wheel and rested one palm on top and one on the stick. "I got this bitch." he said, confident on adrenaline and racial superiority.

Cal popped the glove box and grabbed a mask, and he and Charlie strode across the pavement like it was the streets of Laredo. Charlie kicked open the door unnecessarily and the cowboys charged in brandishing weapons. With the windows rolled down, Terry could hear the muffled shouts and make out the flailing of arms between the window posters for exotic Mex liquors and Budweiser, the king in any language. He wished that he were in there too. The testosterone surge had produced instant facial stubble and he thought about what kind of whore he'd select for the weekend.

It was taking longer than usual for one of these jobs, but that was to be expected, he figured, since there would be a separate safe for the lottery money.

Maybe the greasers were giving them trouble about it, denying and playing dumb. Fucking beaner trash, he thought. Give it up.

A small contingent of civilians was beginning to collect on the sidewalk, somehow aware that something was going down. Spooky how the ethnics were connected like that. A couple of them even turned and looked at Terry who extended his bandaged middle finger to them out the window. He revved the motor as the front door burst open and a masked Charlie emerged pistol in one hand, grocery bag in the other. The door shut again behind him and was instantly painted red in a single blast.

Charlie didn't even turn around. He sprinted across the street and began fumbling with the door handle. Terry stared at the door as the red paint began to slide down, effluvia separating and streaking the glass. The door was flung open again and a stout Mexican woman with a shotgun stepped over the headless corpse of Cal and took aim at the car.

"Go, go, go!" urged Charlie.

"Shit, shit, shit!" countered Terry. The car lurched and died at the same moment Charlie was flung across the seat and into Terry's lap. He was missing the right side of his face. "Shit, motherfuck!" The car started again and Terry pushed Charlie to the other side of the cab. He clipped a parked car and had to use the back of his right hand to clear the blood and hair from the windshield. He succeeded only in smearing it before he had to shift again.

The car lurched a second time, but didn't die and he picked up speed while the back window exploded. A sharp pain in his neck turned warm instantly and he gunned the car. Reaching the windshield again, he scrubbed harder and cleared a window just large enough that he was able to register the streetlight before he struck it.

He woke up in a hospital room. Nurses came in every half hour, police too, but he wasn't speaking yet. He barely registered anyone's presence. Someone snapped their fingers and he followed the sound to a deputy who spoke his name.

"Hickerson. Terry Hickerson. You hear me?"

He must have nodded his head because the next thing he knew they were wheeling him out of the hospital and taking him to the police station. At the station, Terry was seated at a folding table in the break room that doubled for an interrogation space. His head cleared disturbingly quickly as he eyed the Doritos in the vending machine and his stomach bubbled. The deputy came back in the room ten minutes later with two styrofoam cups of weak government coffee. In the light, Terry read his name - Musil.

"What the fuck time is it, Deputy Musil?"

"Two-thirty."

"What time you feature I might get to bed?"

"Just depends on your willingness to cooperate."

"Shit, then I am never going to sleep tonight."

"I just want you to answer a few questions."

"See and I don't want to."

Musil took a sip of coffee and swished it around his mouth. He smiled a sad smile at Terry like he pitied him. It pissed Terry off. Musil leaned back and turned his attention toward the snack machine. He said, "These damn apple pies are making me fat. See, the problem is that coffee is a necessity and what's available here is shit." Musil indicated the coffee in front of Terry which did look poor. "The only thing that makes it drinkable are these sugar bomb 'pastries' and the only thing that makes them tolerable is the bitter-ass coffee."

Musil punched a button and the machine shat out a green paper wrapped apple pie. The policeman peeled it lengthwise, like a banana, and tore off a corner causing white cracks to shoot through the sugar coating. "I bet I could leave one of these in a bowl of milk overnight and it wouldn't be soggy in the morning." He popped the piece into his mouth, took another swig of the coffee and swallowed. "Terry. This has got to be your shit year."

Terry had no objections to that statement.

Amateurs

They were two days into the trip when the train shuddered and the hiss of steam, fighting the brakes applied, caused his bowels to revolt. Through the window, Tip caught a glimpse of a hooded figure standing beside the tracks with a torch. He fought the urge to throw up on his own feet. The Pinkerton across the seat from him chuckled, casually thumbing the cylinder of his Colt and easing back the hammer.

Beside him, Charlie Holland squinted at the night through the glass. "What's going on?" he asked. Tip dreaded hearing the answer.

The Pinkerton winked at them. "Looks like an unscheduled stop."

Tip sat up and pressed his face to the cool

window and spied more torches among the trees. Beside him, Charlie said, "Sonsabitches."

The Pinkerton nodded. "Reckon they gonna wanna talk to you two.

The train came to a full stop and Tip heard loud voices saying his and Charlie's names, but not talking to them. He fought the futile urge to try slipping his manacles and duck beneath his chair. Instead he sent up a silent prayer for quickness, if not justice. Charlie attacked his bonds with admirable verve as he levelled a steady stream of curses under his breath. "Motherfuckers. Sonsa-chink-whore-bitches. Cock-suckin-Lincoln-lovin-rot-ass-mongrels."

The Pinkerton stood and showed Tip his palm. Stay. As if he could run. The detective meant to see them killed no doubt, only not here and now, which made him their only refuge at the moment. Tip looked over his shoulder at him moving to the front of the car and taking a position beside the door. Tip noticed he'd removed a second pistol, tiny. You could conceal it in an eye patch, he thought.

The approaching mob was announced by murmuring from passengers in the other cars and the fierce vibration of violence in the air growing stronger by the second. Charlie began to pull on his chains and Tip's arms were jerked to his right side. Charlie had slipped one boot between his wrists and was attempting to force the cuffs over his hands. "Shit." He wiggled his thumbs trying to make them touch the far sides of his palms. "Don't just sit there, Tip, c'mon, gimme support."

Tip squeezed his eyes shut instead. He listened for the still, small voice of God his mother had told him of, but it was in the storm this time. There was a dull thud against the door, followed by the sharp crack of splintering wood, and three men in potato sack hoods rushed in. The first one called out to them, "On your feet." Charlie paid no heed and pushed with renewed strength. The irons were moving and taking several layers of skin with them.

"Get up," the second hooded man said, "The devil await ye."

A hand reached out and roughly pulled Tip to his feet and another struck him on the mouth and he fell back into his seat. Charlie lay on his back on the floor, absorbing kicks to his ribs, still pushing with his foot between his hands, up in the air.

From behind, the Pinkerton appeared and put

the barrel of his Colt under the chin of the first hood and the lady stinger in the ear of the third man. "The devil gonna have to wait a spell."

The second hooded man stopped reaching for Tip and looked at the Pinkerton. His muffled voice appealed to reason. "We got no strife with you. We only want justice."

"You'll have it. Just gonna have to wait a bit."

"Bullshit," said the voice beneath the first hood, "These boys kilt Bob Manuse plus another posse."

"And they'll hang for it. In Rawlins," said the detective calmly.

"Not good enough. Rawlins awful far from here," said the third man.

"I'm employed by the Union Pacific to bring these men to Rawlins," said the Pinkerton, "That's where they're going. You wanna see them swing, you can buy a ticket like everybody else."

Behind them, a fourth hooded man entered the rail car. "What's the hold up?"

The first man addressed him, "Union Pacific."

The fourth man, clearly the leader said, "Mister, we got no strife with the railroad. Nobody else needs be hurt today." He held up his palms to show that he was unarmed as he approached. "But we will be having justice from thee." The Pinkerton dug the barrels of his guns into the flesh beneath the hoods, causing the first and third man to strain their necks for relief. The fourth man moved cautiously around the huddle of men till he was facing the detective. He bent forward to remove his mask.

What he revealed himself to be was middle-aged, about thirty, and balding. He was in need of a shave, but not unkempt. His features looked soft and healthy, but there was granite behind his eyes. "Sir, my name is Felix Vincent Warden, and I am kin to Robert Manuse by marriage." Here he paused and looked directly at Charlie struggling on the floor and then into the returned gaze of Tip. "I intend to see these die men tonight, I'm sure you understand. Ain't no cause for they to be responsible for no other deaths, but if you don't stand down, we will do what we have to."

The detective sighed and said, "Mr. Warden, I will shoot the very first one of you to put a hand on my prisoners and then I'll shoot one more of you for good measure." He nodded his farewell in a gentlemanly manner and added, "Kindly step the fuck off the train."

Charlie groaned with the effort of straining against his cuffs. His wrists were scraped raw and bleeding, but he'd moved the right side almost over the thumb knuckle, which gave with a crack and a cry from Charlie. His hand slipped through, and he leapt to his feet and lunged at the second man in a hood, who calmly took a single step back and shot Charlie in the belly.

Charlie dropped to Tip's feet. Tip winced and dry-heaved between his knees. The detective, cat-quick, shot the second hooded man up in the fatty part of his arm, with the tiny weapon, causing the man to drop his own gun. The little pop from the toy gun hardly seemed real, but the blood that bubbled out of the flesh wound was convincing.

Charlie lay curled on the floor, cursing and gargling blood, while the man who shot him sat in an empty seat and grabbed at the hole in his arm. "Would one of you shoot that son of a bitch!" he said.

The Pinkerton re-cocked the lady stinger, and the hooded men flinched and turned their heads slightly to Felix Warden who had taken on a purplish color. "Now listen here, you fancy son of a bitch –" he said.

The Pinkerton fired a shot, from the Colt this time, through the ceiling right beside the first hooded man's ear. The man descended to the floor clutching at his head through the hood and the Pinkerton levelled the Colt into the second man's face.

Below them, the first man had pulled the hood off of his head and was screaming, "Shot my fuckin ear out! Shot my fuckin ear dead! Can't fuckin hear anything!" His eyes were wide and he was looking from hood to hood for recognition that he was indeed saying something. Receiving none, he scrambled to his feet and ran out the door.

From outside the train there was a commotion of voices calling for Warden to tell them what was happening. From the next car more men could be heard approaching the door. The Pinkerton told Felix Warden, "Tell them to stand down or I'll shoot the first one through the door."

Warden commanded in a level voice, "Stay back. Do not come in. Everything's under control."

"That's good, Felix, now –"

Warden continued, his voice raised, "But you boys hear any more guns, you come in shooting!"

Tip knelt beside Charlie on the floor. He tore the

hem from his companion's clothing and tried to staunch the flow of blood with Charlie's own shirt. His partner looked up at him with hatred in his eyes. "Why didn't you help me, you fuckin coward?"

Tip gagged on the smells of blood and vomit mixing and filling the car. "Shh, Charlie, don't talk, now."

Charlie tried to spit at him, but only drooled bloody saliva down his chin. "Chickenshit backshooter," he managed. "Never shoulda hooked up with such a yellow-ass-mutt. Fuckin left you to die's what I shoulda done."

The detective looked at Warden, disappointed as if with a child. He started to speak, "Felix, I believe we can work something out." Felix Vincent Warden waited for his offer. The Pinkerton looked first at Tip wiping a string of drool from his chin and Charlie bleeding and bubbling shit all over the car floor. "I'll give you one of em."

* * *

Supported between two men, Charlie Holland was led off the train into a circle of other hoods and train passengers come out to watch, gathered around a telegraph pole. Two men were struggling with fashioning a noose and Charlie slumped on the ground waiting for them to finish. Felix Warden called out for haste, "Git him up before he bleeds to death."

The Pinkerton poked Tip in the ribs with his Colt. Tip stood from his seat and walked to the front of the car, watching the mob through the windows, feeling a mix of gratitude and shame that Charlie was dying and not himself. His captor and savoir led him all the way to the engine where the driver regarded them warily before turning his attention again to the lynching. The Pinkerton spoke, "What are you waiting for, get this heap moving."

The engineer didn't look at him. "Can't. Rails blocked." The detective put his head out and inspected the track for himself.

"So get your men out there to clear it."

"Pinch it. Let 'em watch." He turned to look at Tip. "Shoulda let 'em take both."

"Ain't your concern. Just get us moving along, pronto."

"Case you hadn't noticed, half my passengers are out there to watch. I ain't leaving without them. Why don't you just go back to your seat, you don't wanna see it for yourself?"

The Pinkerton motioned for Tip to step off the train and he did. Tip fell to his knees when he landed, and the detective put a hand under his arm to help him to his feet. "If you don't want to die with your friend tonight, you'd best help me clear this track. Soon as he's stretched, they're gonna want you."

They worked together, clearing away the barricade the mob had hastily placed across the track. They'd lit a fire in front to make it more visible and simultaneously obscure the shoddy obstacle they'd erected. The blaze was reduced to a few smouldering, mostly smoking, patches of timber. It was primarily still-green tree branches and even the trunks of a half dozen saplings lying in a pile.

"Amateurs," said the Pinkerton.

A loud cry rang out when Charlie was lifted to his feet and assisted atop a patiently waiting ass. Charlie began to vocalize his final thoughts. They mostly consisted of objects and animals those gathered round were advised to fornicate with and how he wished he'd killed more of them. He claimed further that Robert Manuse had died like a coward, begging for his life and even sucking on Charlie's cock for mercy before he'd shot him.

It wasn't true. They'd been holed up in a cave for a week, hiding out from a botched train job, when the posse had found them. Tip had been taking a shit across the way when the popping sounds of gunfire had sent him scrambling down the hill, goodbye forever to the gang.

He'd been a road agent before joining up with up with the McKinny-Jan gang that'd failed to stop a train outside Rawlins. He'd been party to bushwhacking and rustling and cheating at cards, but it was an attempted robbery that had brought this end. He and Charlie had busted up the tracks ten miles outside town, but a UP lineman discovered the damaged rails and had the train stopped before it got anywhere near them.

Union Pacific had a posse formed and out before nightfall with an inflated bounty placed on them, and the gang had disappeared up into the mountains. A week after, he'd heard the shooting and began his pilgrimage east without even stopping to wipe his ass. Weeks later, he'd chanced upon Charlie again at a saloon they both knew in Kansas City and heard confirmation from him the tale of the shootout he'd read about in newspapers. A railroad detective and a citizen were killed in the ambush, and Jensen and Collins shot dead from their own company. McKinny and Jan had escaped far as he knew.

Charlie claimed pure dumb luck had saved him that day and that fate had brought them back together that night. He bought Tip a round and a whore and later claimed innocence and bewilderment when they'd found the Pinkerton waiting for them in the bath house.

Upon arrest, the detective had advised quiet if they wanted to survive the trip back to Rawlins, but apparently word had got out they'd been apprehended. Telegraph messages outran any horse, carriage or train. Newspapers were probably printing stories of their capture already. Fuckin Charlie'd testify to that much.

* * *

His hands bound behind him and the noose placed around his neck, Charlie was made to sit atop the miserable looking ass who could not then be coaxed to move. Two men pulled on the stubborn animal's reigns and a third pushed from behind while Charlie abused them with words.

Finally the reluctant ass took three steps and then stopped, leaving Charlie, stretched taut, holding onto the animal's hind quarters with his heels and wriggling his head in the rope, until one of the men brushed his feet off. Charlie swung low, his feet missing the ground by inches. He made a wide arc and as he swung back, he kicked his heels in a rhythm that added to his momentum. He was finally able to grab the telegraph pole with his heels and holding himself still, wriggled his head with savage determination until one of the mob knocked his feet loose and Charlie commenced to swinging again. With each swing, the knot slipped a hair. At the zenith of the fourth swing, he fell through the noose and landed on his back. The rope, which had torn both of his ears away from his head, swung empty, garnished with his right extremity and a long strand of hair. The left fell in the dirt. Charlie lay on the ground, heaving wet, broken breaths.

The Pinkerton shook his head. "Amateurs."

They had cleared away the barrier and stood with the engineer who chuckled at the spectacle. Tip couldn't take his eyes off his partner who was left lying in the dust, in shock and too raw and scraped about the neck to cry out, while the mob hurried to fashion a better noose.

Felix Vincent Warden motivated his mob to "make a good one this time." And after a spell, the second version was fitted and cinched tight on Charlie's ragged throat. He slumped, barely upright, atop the mule who'd been cajoled back to the spot beneath the crossbeam of the telegraph pole. Again when the animal was slapped it refused to budge and the same three men set about seducing it away from its spot, but to no avail. Of a sudden, a fourth man stepped forward and shot the dumb animal behind its ear. The mule fell to the earth and Charlie Holland dropped with it, but stopped short of the ground.

Again, he kicked with both his feet and again he managed to get a swing going, but Felix Harden called for a stop to that and two men grabbed his kicking feet and tugged without syncopation until there was a pop. Charlie stopped squirming, went slack and vacated what remained in his bowels.

The gathered crowd became nearly as still as Charlie, whose only motion now was prompted by a dry and dusty wind carrying the smell of him back toward Tip. The Pinkerton urged the engineer to prepare to leave and as the onlookers began filing silently back aboard the train, he and Tip stood up front with the driver watching Charlie tilt and sway.

Tip realized that the detective had been wrong. Charlie's messy exit had left the mob uninterested in his blood and they pulled away without further incident. Several of the hooded men even set about clearing away brush still remaining on the track and others gallantly assisted ladies back to their seats. As he retook his own seat in the otherwise empty car, Tip stared out the window, but the light inside obscured the night and he was left with his own reflection to study.

They were still six hours from Rawlins and maybe six days to execution. The Pinkerton seemed to read his thoughts and offered, "You never know, sometimes a judge gets sick or lost making the trip and another one's gotta be called in. Could take weeks."

Tip considered that as the train pulled away. He glanced back for a final look at Charlie and the detective snorted. "You don't owe that cocksucker nothing. Gave you up five minutes after we caught him in the hills outside Rawlins. Said he knew you had an uncle in Kentucky, figured you'd be headed that way." Tip took the information stoically. It made sense. The Pinkerton watched the subtle changes in Tip's expression and nodded in agreement. "Fuck him. He deserved it."

The Adversary

And it entered into his body like water, and like oil into his bones.
– Psalm109:18

Since word of the spread of Tecumseh's scourge, its destination and inevitable path made obvious, panic had seized the wise and charlatanism the foolish. Repentance, as ever, sucked hind teat.

The witch had been holding ceremonies. Sacrifices. Poultry mostly. She blessed and hexed for a fee and she'd send and deliver messages across the Stygian chasms separating worlds. All of her arts were brought over from the Dark Continent and she practiced in the woods under penalty of death by the

Law of Moses, which the Reverend Chalfont Avery was charged with upholding now in the face of Armageddon. He had been present at her execution, a willing and enthusiastic participant, but the kicking feet of the blasphemer brought not the warmth of God to his soul, so they torched her home to mirror the flames of Hades and on them he warmed his hands.

The fervor for purging had hit an all time high by Avery's measure and every arcane law of superstition was dusted off and seemed to shine with special relevance to the here and now because where was God? The Northern Philistines were paving a scorched path directly to them through autumnal Georgia; a season of wrath to match any Biblical account and Avery, try as he might to conjure himself Moses descending Sinai and meeting the orgy 'round the golden heifer, could not escape the thought that he was merely Balaam leaving behind his conversant ass and extending a hand of brotherhood to the Angel of Death, I have started without you.

When Chalfont was a youth, and the Apostle Naaman Mosley had first called him into the service of an acolyte, he had felt the Spirit's breath in his own lungs as if awakened from dormancy. The Apostle had recognized the gift in Chalfont, called it out of him and set into motion a great and dynamic ministry. He had performed signs and wonders and prophesied, cast out dark spirits and baptized thousands. They had come to him from a hundred miles in every direction for the words of God that fell from his lips and the touch of power in his hands and Chalfont Avery's name was known all the way from Athens to New Orleans.

But now he was empty.

The authority that had coursed through his speech and actions, that he had eventually mistaken for his own and then behaved in such a manner with encouragement from a silver-tongued politician whose appointment to the state senate Chalfont had helped secure with enthusiastic endorsements and inspired editorials printed in the papers, that authority was null. Once established, the partnership with the government man was influential and lucrative, but in retrospect Chalfont had been intoxicated with infallibility in tandem with the way the sway of his gift had faltered. But no one saw it when he had led a prayer on the battlefield at

Chickamauga and thoughts of his own political office would not have seemed outlandish, though by Kennesaw Mountain he was mostly gassy fervor and untethered moral authority.

* * *

That untethering had come up in the public rebuke given to his face in front of his own congregation by the Apostle who'd traveled all the way to Athens to deliver it. But by that time his spiritual dipsomania had claimed Avery's senses and he was not inclined to listen to the contrary and jealousy-fueled ranting of the dispossessed and failed. Now, the Apostle's last words to him hung between his ears filling the depression where once the Spirit had resided and spoken an unstopped spring of wisdom for him to translate into language and wield his flesh around. "He has removed his Spirit from you and changed your name to Ichabod."

The Apostle had collapsed afterward. His body dropped like Ananias or Sapphira right there in the sanctuary, and he had taken the voice of God with him. From the pulpit Chalfont had watched him fall and felt closed inside with the void by the ornate, church doors as soon as his mentor had expired. He had known the sensation at once, though it was terribly and utterly new. Soon he would see Sheol and know not the bosom of Abraham. He was a goat now, and would no more be so had he horns protruding from his forehead.

Members of the church had rushed to the Apostle's side. A man named Barnabus had knelt and taken the Apostle's crown into his lap. He had placed his own head near the peaceful face on the floor, then looked up and confirmed to all what was apparent to Avery, The Apostle was dead.

Chalfont had retreated immediately to his hometown of Gilboa sighting grief over the death of his dearest friend and had no sooner arrived than the wrath of God had rained in cannonade fire upon Atlanta and the faithful in exile had changed its significance from New Jerusalem to Babylon in their pleas and railings against the tide of reckoning washing toward them from the north and west.

The territorial Marshal had arrived at his door with a proposition - clear the scrub, dispose of the brush and the fire will not consume us for His judgment falls on the just and the unjust alike, but while Lot's wife became salt, even Nineveh was spared – and Chalfont had been deputized and slain with fervor to catch the neglectful eye of the God of Abraham, Isaac and Jacob, but His jealousy was attached to the Babylonian whore with her mouth round Chalfont, and He remained aloof.

Wrath seemed preferable to indifference and Chalfont had set himself up to be noticed.

* * *

On the first morning of the third week since his return, he woke with a start well before dawn, fleeing the same vision that had pursued him through his sleep ever since they'd stretched the African witch. In the dream, she'd addressed him as Simon Sorcerer and not Simon Peter. Worse, he had answered her as if it were his given and accepted name. He woke now, slick with dread, and collapsed there on his knees beside the bed. He cried out to the power of God, but received no deliverance and no answer. He rocked and heaved and hyperventilated in his fervent pleading for a divine word, but none came.

At last he rose, stumbled out of his house and crossed the packed earth to his stable, fed and dressed his mare for light travel. Within the hour streaks of grey had shot through the cracks in the black and he discerned the final crest of the hills that led to the place where she'd lived and died.

The tall grass gave way to loamy pathways from the dismantled livestock pens to the blackened place where the cabin had previously stood. An acrid, smoky smell hung in the air still, held low in the atmosphere as if it were a place that the wind avoided. His horse whined and Chalfont dismounted. He led her to the outermost edges of fence and loosely tethered her there, before continuing toward the tree at the center of the property.

The fire that had reduced the cabin to a collection of charred sticks huddled like spent matches about a roughly rectangular lot had not touched the tree, which stood defiantly an iridescent green even in winter against the scorched, ashen earth and bloody haze of sunrise spreading across the sky. The tree's shade was vast and inky and once beneath, he trembled slightly. Near the trunk, suspended a meter off the ground, the nubs of her feet, ravaged by wild beasts, were just visible.

He remembered now the way she'd cried out upon seeing him. Her bewilderment at the transaction gone sideways turning to stark fear and then bright, black anger, outraged by the devil's betrayal. She cursed him in a dozen heathen languages and licked blasphemy at him betwixt her fingers before he'd claimed her tongue. The posse dropped their pretense and held her down and stripped away her clothes. She'd struggled beneath them, in agony or ecstasy it was difficult to differentiate. Franklin had clapped his hand over her mouth to halt the profanity and he'd looked over his shoulder in hesitation at Chalfont, who'd nodded, then turned his back on her as they'd sawed away at the pale, flapping appendage, finally claiming it in a tug that nearly choked her dead before she could be hung proper. The meat had fallen beneath the spot she'd kicked above while the horse tugged and eventually left her levitating over, angry tendrils atwitch, searching for a suitable spot in which to plant themselves and grow again.

As he approached her now, he caught movement in the circle of yellowing grass beneath her corpse as if the tongue had found purchase and sprouted. What he saw when he was near enough to discern stopped his breath halfway in so that he choked when he remembered the mechanics of breathing again five seconds later. An abominable trinity of cottonmouths writhing there, tangled in a blind sex frenzy. So thick was their lust that they were not disturbed by him and did not yield their ground, and he was forced to kick them with his boot from the spot. They landed in three separate spaces six feet apart and were immediately released from her spell. They slid and slipped away, seemingly ignorant and uninterested in what had preceded. He looked up at her face, eyes gone with the birds, fingers curled into hooks. He took out his knife to cut her down thinking to bury her and end the tormenting nightmares, but as soon as he'd laid his hands upon her body, he swooned.

* * *

There was a pressure on his right side so that Chalfont turned his head and beheld the fingers of his hand wrapped tightly around a squirming serpent which coiled likewise around his arm and attached itself by teeth to his throat. A smell as if crimson had an odor crept up his nostrils and lodged in his brainpan and he heard tongues that he could not interpret. He stood atop a hill and saw from the western horizon a spill of smoke rolling over the land and the hungry lick of flames, emissaries of the inferno they announced blacking out the sun. From this advance a sound eventually arrived, percussive and predatory. The beat a rumbling, grinding rhythm like the turning of a great mill that split off into scores of separate swells becoming a crescendo.

* * *

Upon waking he saw that the body lay beside him in the grass and that it was, even then, being fed upon by bold scavengers who took no notice of him. With a start, he rolled to his feet and decided to let the animals claim her. It would be peace enough as her type was likely ever to know and if it brought him a restful night of sleep and a firming up of his bowels, so much the better.

* * *

Through the night he slipped under sleep a dozen times and came up again clutching his breast a few minutes later. His attempts to shirk the visions were futile and his efforts with the witch's body in vain. Even if he had succeeded in burying her, he knew it would have been fruitless. He cried in frustration and seethed in anger at his heavenly father who had abandoned him. The day found him limp and spent, gaunt and so pale that he had been turned away by the gaggle of terrified collaborators he led. They agreed he looked like death and they would go the day without a lynching.

He had retired back to his cot where he'd fallen into a more substantial sleep, which produced a dream that he was not able to escape this time.

* * *

He stood in the pulpit before his congregation waiting for the Apostle to speak. But his mentor stood mute in the aisle, glaring at him with the perspicacious sight of The Spirit. Chalfont thought to appease him with words, but felt his insides shudder and a weak belch escape his mouth accompanied by a smell like spoiled eggs. The Apostle imperceptibly flared his nostrils and tilted his head. The intensity of his gaze Chalfont could feel on his face like breath. A tickle on his upper lip caused him to touch his fingers to his visage. Upon taking his hand away he studied it, and found that there had begun a nosebleed. He tried to sniff back the trickle of blood and then clutched at his nostrils. He then began to blow trying to dislodge the obstruction inside. After three brief attempts to clear the passage he felt the object work its way out of his airway and pinched it between his forefinger and thumb as soon as it had cleared the orifice. He saw the Apostle drop his gaze and heard the congregation gasp as he pulled the worm from his proboscis. He held it up to inspect and it began to twist and wriggle in increasing agitation.

Chalfont dropped the creature and gagged. He coughed and spit three pale maggots onto the floor beside the worm. The front three rows of the church stood and the Apostle turned and began to slowly walk out of the room. Chalfont cried out after him, but no words came, only a great slug which he extricated with his hand and cast away with such force that it rocked the wood podium he stood behind. A woman from the flock screamed and the Apostle disappeared through the chapel doors which shut with such certainty behind him that everyone in the congregation had been startled and turned around to regard them.

A steady and increasingly heavy procession of crawling things erupted from Chalfont's mouth and clogged his nose and trickled from his ears, though he remained standing and never stopped trying to speak. By the time a great serpent had slid from his anus and was poking its head out the leg of his trousers the church was in an uproar. Women were crying, men were cursing and some were trying to force open the doors that would not budge.

Though unable to breath for the flow of herpetological beasts from every aperture of his body, Chalfont began to laugh.

* * *

It turned to sobbing as soon as he woke.

The witch's house had a Persimmon tree growing right through the middle, a hole in the floor and roof, and Avery wondered at its significance. Set into the woods in no cleared area either by laziness or design, there was a small vegetable garden preceding the door and separated from the forest only by a creaking gate, which Chalfont entered through, announcing his presence to the seer, though he wondered if that were necessary.

He'd left his shiny star at home and worn unfamiliar clothes in an effort to hide his identity. A man of God by reputation still, and a semi-deputized vigilante, he was more concerned with concealing himself from the hoodoo darky for fear she'd clam up and refuse his patronage than that some Christian citizen would be scandalized by his consorting with evil spirits. His desperate need to touch a spiritual dimension again had brought him this low; demons and niggers, but the ethereal plain it would be.

The front door opened while he was yet five strides away, and he beheld the Negress, impossible to say how old, but a handsome woman with a healthy build. She was dressed in rags, but they were clean and her hair was occupied in twisted together ropes and given to adventurous trajectories, around her face and over her shoulders, once sprouted. She tucked her chin and cocked her hip slightly, resting her left hand upon its sturdy form and gave him a look that was part enticement and part challenge. Chalfont stopped his advance and held up his right hand in greeting. She gave him a good once over and glanced about the woods quickly before jutting her chin out and addressing him. "What you want?"

Chalfont reached slowly into his breast pocket and withdrew his wallet, stuffed with Confederate currency and showed it to her.

The African scoffed. "Ain worth shit nohow." Chalfont smiled and pulled out a bag of gold and silver coins from about his waist and tossed it to her. The woman caught his pouch and inspected it disinterestedly. "What you want?"

Chalfont paused. What exactly did he want?

He settled on, "I want to talk to God."

The witch laughed a low and pitying chuckle, and Chalfont felt anger rising in him. "Go home and pray, Christian. Jesus be listen to you." She tossed the coin purse back to him and began to close the door, but Chalfont stepped forward and put his foot in the gap. The door stopped on his boot and she increased the pressure, but he held his place. When he saw her eyes again, the change was marked. Gone was any pretense at demureness, her teeth were bared and her voice was a hiss. "Go away, Christian."

But Chalfont pushed back, "I want to talk to the dead."

The woman continued to push, "Is an abomination, dey kill me for it."

Finally, Chalfont withdrew his foot and the door slammed in his face, but he did not leave. "I want to pay you for it." He listened to the still night. "Please." Suddenly, the anger was gone and it was replaced with desperate fear again. His eyes watered and his breath caught in his chest. "Please, I have to."

The door creaked and opened a few inches. Chalfont stood still, holding his breath. From inside the tiny house her voice came to him as if from the depths of a cavernous space. "Come in, then. Close the door behind."

The cabin did seem much larger inside than out,

even crowded as it was with exotic and profane paraphernalia. Pairs of chicken's feet tied together hung from nails in the wall, folded paper parchments of ground spices that he could not name and at least four different types of mossy vegetation hung in cascading formations from pots suspended from the low ceiling.

A modest fire barely burned in the corner, but filled the space with a pungent smoke that made Chalfont's eyes water and his breathing deliberate. "Sit down," came the voice, but he still couldn't place her in the room. He did find a seat fashioned from a tree stump and sat upon it before a small, but heavy wooden table. Chalfont turned his head to find her and saw nothing behind him, but when he faced forward again, she was seated opposite him on the other side of the table. "Now den," she took his hand in hers and the touch was like ice that traveled up his arm and through his torso putting out a fever that he had not even noticed was there. "Tell me who it is you wan to speak wit."

"Naaman Mosley."

If she recognized the Apostle's name, she did not show it, only concentrated on his touch for a full minute. Then she selected some dried leaves and ground them into a powder. She removed a water pot from its place over the fire and strained it through them, making a tea, which she offered to him and told him to drink. He did. Chalfont had never tasted anything so bitter, but the warmth of it seemed good in his stomach. He felt a ball of calm, ringed-round with a coat of prickly sensitivity begin to grow inside him. He sprouted goose flesh and an erection after a few minutes.

She sang softly or chanted a mumbly, indistinct parade of sounds that made no sense to him, but held an atonal cadence that he fixed on and learned and went with instinctually, anticipating its rise and fall. She continued repeating her song and watched him closely for some time, and he tried to do the same and hold her steady in his gaze, but she kept shifting suddenly to the far edges of his periphery, slipping the grasp of his gaze, though he was quite certain she was sitting still. Finally, he bent over and vomited a thin, black stream of tea and bile onto the earthen floor and when he sat up again, she closed her eyes and hummed a single low note.

She held that note for an impossible term,

increasing the volume and intensity until her eyes popped open to reveal only white beneath her ocular hoods. The humming stopped and she began to hyperventilate with quick, shallow, noisy breaths. And then the voice of the Apostle came forth from her lips.

"Who is calling me?"

* * *

Chalfont didn't know what to say. Finally he stuttered, "It's me, Naaman. It is Chalfont."

The witch's face contorted in a mask of terror and she produced a strangled cry, which she held quite independent from the Apostle's voice. "Why have you disturbed me?"

Chalfont quaked and fell to his knees. He pressed his forehead into the floor and cried. "I am so greatly distressed. The enemy advances unabated, sacking and burning and destroying everything and God's spirit has left me and does not answer."

Now the witch formed words of her own with great effort. She hissed at Chalfont, "You have tricked me and come to kill me."

"No," said Chalfont.

"Yes," she said. You are the one murdering

mediums."

The Apostle spoke to the woman through her very own faculties. "No harm will come to you on account of this man. He has been brought here to degrade himself by the hand of God."

Chalfont sobbed. "Why? Please help me. Tell me what I should do."

The witch's voice was now merely a faint whine underneath the sound of the Apostle. "You should prepare yourself to die, Chalfont. You have made yourself the adversary of God and He has considered you chaff and delivered you into the hands of your enemy. Tomorrow you will surely die."

Then the Apostle left. The witch's eyes rolled back into her face and she looked at Chalfont with terror and rage. The terror receded some and the rage evaporated at the sight of Chalfont lying on his side on the floor, his head resting in a pool of snot and tears. She got up from where she sat and began to prepare food.

He emptied all his strength to cry in ten minutes and lay quietly awake on the floor until the woman brought him the meal she'd prepared. "Sit up," she said with the gentle firmness of a mother. Chalfont obeyed and she fed him spoonfuls of a brothy soup that sharpened his senses to the point that he finished feeding himself.

When he had eaten enough, she helped him to his horse and once astride, she said, "I'm sorry."

"For what?" asked Chalfont.

"I'm sorry that it wasn't better news."

* * *

When he returned home, he did not stable his horse, but set her loose to do as she pleased. He spent that night, his last on earth, listening to the trickle of scout riders passing and prophesying the great current of the devil's flood.

* * *

With the dawn came smoke from the fields of his neighbor and the great creeping swarm of Shermanites, their image slippery through the heat. Avery set his own barn alight and strode toward their army with his a pistol in his hands, his bible left to the flames. As they began to separate into distinction and he discerned the countenance of their fore, he called out, "Blessed is he who comes in the name of the Lord," before shooting himself through the brain.

Viscosity

"You country boys are fucked up. All I'm sayin."

"Like you popped your cherry in the prom queen."

"Far as you know."

"Get the fuck outta here."

"Nah, he's got sisters."

"What are you implying?"

"Jus saying. Why would you need to get creative? All that natural snatch at hand."

"Creative? That what you're calling it?"

"What else?"

"Like I said, you country boys are fucked up."

"Hear that, Mike? Says we're fucked up."

"I hear that, Tom. Sounds like a jealous man,

lashing out."

"Whatever."

"You're right, Mike. Sounds like a man thinking, 'Damn, I didn't even eat the shit'."

"Didn't."

"See? Never had fried chicken either, huh?"

"Just cause you some seriously disturbed hillbilly don't give you cause to attack my momma's cooking."

"The night is young, my friends, the night is young."

"Keep it up, you'll see how young this night is. Keep heading that direction you'll see real quick this night is fucking geriatric."

"Sounds like a man tantalized."

"Sounds like a man uncomfortable with an awakening."

"Check please."

"Oh take it easy. There's no judgment here."

"I tell you what, I will not be that drunk tonight or ever. White people all like you? 'Cause that might explain a thing or two."

"People all like us, period. Not as smart, all of em, but made of the same stuff. Including you, my man."

"First I ever heard of it and I'm no innocent."

"Okay, okay. Then what?"

"You askin?"

"You heard me."

"Just so y'all know you're some sick motherfuckers, I'll answer. Tennis ball cans."

"Wha-?"

"No!"

"How exactly?"

"No way. Got like a three inch diameter."

"Yeah."

"Do you wanna hear, or not?"

"So explain."

"For a master race, y'all some slow sons of bitches. Got yourself a can-"

"Like a tin can with the pressure and shit?"

"Yeah, they got pressure, but all the ones I ever seen were plastic."

"Amazed you saw any in your neighborhood."

"Racist motherfucker. I could take you any day."

"Well I never played that pansy bullshit."

"Yeah. You must've got yourself beat the hell up every day."

"Not for tennis."

VISCOSITY

"No?"

"No. We played at night. In the summer, at the public courts, after the lights would go out around ten. My boy Maleek and me? We'd go up with a couple of beat up old rackets we got at the pawn shop and collect all the balls the white folks left. Then we'd soak 'em with lighter fluid and -whoosh- ... was like tracers or some shit."

"Bull-"

"No, really. You could hold it in your hand and everything. Didn't burn, 'casue the flame always goes up. Sometimes we'd just play catch with our bare hands."

"Huh."

"Burned a long ass time too."

"Should have that on ESPN. Smokeball."

"Yeah, then the loser has to fuck the can."

"Explain that, now."

"Y'all making me lose my train of thought."

"How far away was this court?"

"I don't know, ten blocks?"

"What does it matter?"

"Just wondering how important smokeball was to you guys."

"Who cares?"

"Yeah, man why you care?"

"I wouldn't walk three blocks for tennis."

"Nah, man, but you'd scoot your narrow white ass all over the pumpkin patch for a date."

"So were you like always gettin a boner watchin Jimmy Connors?"

"Didn't watch that shit. Shit. Just 'cause I play don't mean I'm obsessed. Got better things to do with my time than watch people in white shorts-"

"So, after an exhausting night of smokeball and a fucking epic journey home-"

"-you crawl into bed and reach underneath for your tennis ball can Cindy-"

"Pam."

"Coffey. Hell yeah."

"Okay it was stuffed right?"

"Stuffed?"

"With like bread crumbs and savory seasoning?"

"Tissue. Kleenex. And generously lubed with uh-"

"Vaseline."

"Sometimes. Or any sort of moisturizer."

"I used vegetable oil sometimes."

"On fruit?"

"No. With my hand. Smell made me hungry though. Was a little disconcerting."

"Dude, one time I used some serious poison."

"What?"

"No shit. My mom was out of the house and I was making a night of it. Jacking off with all the different stuff in the house."

"Once with a bar of soap-"

"Yeah-"

"Ever use the hand pump stuff?"

"Yeah, plus like Dawn dish soap and shit."

"What else?"

"Uh peanut butter and jelly."

"Together?"

"Yeah, plus my dog helped out."

"No!"

"Didn't really help, though. Tongue was all rough. But he was hard to discourage. He really liked peanut butter."

"You sick fuck."

"Oh like you're not a cantaloupe cuddler."

"What poison?"

"Was some sort of furniture polish."

"No shit."

"Burned like shit, but good viscosity."

"Vis- what?"

"Too bad."

"You get sick?"

"Yeah. Felt pretty shitty for a couple days."

"Tell your moms?"

"No. Like I gotta add to her worries. Just curled up and told her my stomach hurt. Burned when I pissed and I'll tell you what else... My dickhead swelled up like an arrowhead or some shit."

"Yo, me too."

"What?"

"For real. Sometimes when the cans weren't tight enough and I was using a shit load of moisturizer I'd squeeze my dick like it was a venomous snake. I mean both hands all slippery and smooth by now turning white trying to choke that thing and then afterward shit would swell up just like he said."

"Freaked me out."

"Me too the first time."

"What'd you do?"

"Nothin. Freaked out. Just looked at it all the time."

"And?"

"Nothin. After a while, like the next day, it'd go back to normal."

"You didn't tell your parents or nothin?"

"Shit, no. Learned my lesson with all that. One time I was looking at my asshole in the mirror-"

"Don't tell me that."

"When?"

"Yesterday."

"No, was like ten years old. Everything was about your asshole then, remember?"

"No."

"No."

"Liars. Anyway, was looking at it and looked a little y'know? Lumpy."

"Lumpy?"

"Y'know, normal. Anyway, I thought I had a hemorrhoid. I'd just heard about hemorrhoids, right? And I thought, oh shit it's a roid and I go running downstairs, crying and tell my parents I think I've got a hemorrhoid."

"No."

"Yeah. No. Bad news. Yeah, got a year's worth of sideways glances from that, so no I didn't tell my mom I had a fuckin' huge swollen arrowhead cock."

"Maybe you should have."

"Shut up."

"Just sayin maybe you wouldn't had to start violating produce."

"Still say, you don't know what you missed."

"Yeah, sounded crazy to me at first, too, but hey kudos for peer pressure."

"Wait, peer pressure?"

"Yeah, not like it was my idea."

"You telling me it was what? A watermelon gang bang?"

"..."

"You're not-"

"I guess you could draw some parallels."

"I am so through with your ass."

"Yeah I don't know."

"You too?"

"Yeah, well it was my idea. I never did that shit with nobody."

"Me either. Not like we all held hands and wiped each other off or nothing."

"So, you're just hanging out with your buddies in this totally hetero kinda way and somebody says, I know a melon who goes all the way?"

"No, it was a party."

"No chicks?"

"Actually there were a lot of girls there."

"Nigga wha?"

"Yeah was sort of a macho thing. One guy picks up this uh cantaloupe and starts drawing on it with a marker. Makes a face with like colored eyes and everything and big, y'know sexy lips? Anyway, he's a bit annoying, going around the room trying to get in to conversations with the melon and other people like a ventriloquist or some shit?"

"Drunk?"

"I don't even think so. Drama guy or whatever. Anyway, starting to piss people off, which of course means he's gotta step it up, really get in people's faces, 'cause that's the way they're wired. So this one guy, big football guy or something, grabs it and kisses it and pushes it into his crotch and starts moaning. Everybody laughs, then he tosses it to his buddy across the room, who takes out a knife and cuts out a hole where the mouth is and this guy-"

"No!"

"-stands up and drops his pants-"

"Oh my god."

"-and actually sticks his dick in there and like pumps away, tosses it to another guy and everybody, especially the girls, y'know? They're cheering like he's a sex god or at least-"

"So the next guy?"

"Yeah, of course. I mean, I don't know about you, but I was so desperate to make an impression on girls back then and here they were, a room full of 'em fucking cheering for guys to whip it out and fuck the melon."

"Damn."

"You climax?"

"Hell no, I was so nervous, I could barely get hard enough to get it in there, but it was such a rush, y'know everybody watching and once it was in was like, well damn that's not bad."

"So you became like, what a serial rapist of vegetables?"

"Tried it all."

"Yeah I didn't stop at one type of fruit either. My mom thought I was some kinda health nut one summer. Was always going to the store and coming home with y'know healthy shit voluntarily."

VISCOSITY

"Yeah, my parents were not about to look too closely, either. Before that all I wanted to eat was like McNuggets and shit."

"Yeah, and I didn't start with fruit you know? Saw this porno once with my friend and there's this bitch gettin' turned inside fucking out doing lez stuff and my friend he looks at me and says, just offhand, like how it kinda looks like a twinkie getting split open."

"What?"

"Were you high?"

"No, I know it didn't make much sense, but kinda stuck with me and one day I'm all alone and there was always shit like that in the house-"

"Parents didn't love your ass, huh?"

"What can I say, there was always sugary cereal too."

"Motherfucker, you know what I had to chew every miserable shitty morning? Shredded Wheat. No sugar, no honey or some Sweet'n'Low suburban white folk shit. Shredded fucking Wheat or sometimes Grape Nuts."

"Granola."

"Your ass's got nothing to complain about

granola. Some tasty hippy shit, man."

"Not the serious shit. It's just like nuts and rocks and corn stalks, little dirt sprinkled on if you're lucky."

"Anyway, took out a knife and opened a Twinkie, just laid my dick in the creamy center."

"Shit how tiny is your dick?"

"I was a little kid. Anyway, I was just starting. Next time I used two. Made like a sandwich out of it... Never looked back. Took a while to find fruit, but you know what innovation I'm most proud of?"

"Real pussy?"

"Microwave."

"Yes! Shit yes!"

"Popped it in the microwave first and got that warm feeling."

"Seriously degenerate shit."

"Was dangerous though."

"No doubt. Sometimes I'd blow shit up before I could fuck it."

"No it was worse."

"Like how?"

"Well I was fucking every kind of food I could think of and one Thanksgiving it hits me, duh, mashed potatoes."

"Hell yeah."

"Except there's no uh grip y'know?"

"Not like a twinkie."

"Exactly."

"Except Twinkies didn't work that well. Fell apart pretty quick."

"But just putting it in a bowl once with like melting butter. Had to find a way. Thought about it for a while then was like dude - baked potato. So, popped one in the microwave for a couple minutes-"

"Think I know where this is-"

"Had to get like an oven mitt-"

"Idiot."

"Yeah. Really burned the shit outta my dick."

"No."

"How bad?"

"Blistered."

"Oh!"

"Peeling."

"Ssss!"

"Let me guess, didn't tell your parents?"

"No, put some Vaseline on it, but-"

"That's like a heat conductor-"

"Yeah, had to wash it off immediately in cold water but I found some Preparation H."

"Scar?"

"No, still got a pretty ass dick."

"What a relief."

"No doubt."

"Mine's ugly as fuck."

Nolte

"So, the show-"

"The show?"

"Yeah, the show, right? It's got uh...Nolte-"

"Nick Nolte?"

"There are others? Yeah Nick Nolte and uh um the other uh"

"Sam Elliot?"

"Shut up"

"The cowboy guy, right?"

"Shut up. No. No Sam Elliot"

"'Cause he's great, you ever see Hi Lo Country? No mustache- OW!"

"I said shut up. No. No Sam Elliot, no Kiefer Sutherland. It's not a showcase of whiskey and cigarette voices. Listen. Sorry about that, but you sometimes... Just listen."

"Yeah, okay"

"The show, then... It's got uh"

"Nolte"

"Motherfucker do not interrupt me again. I'm losing my- Yes, Nolte and what's his, uh the Spanish guy from uh-"

"Rueben Blades"

"No"

"Antonio Banderas"

"No, shut the fuck up"

"John Legui-"

"No, uh the the the the bull."

"Gravano? He's not Span-"

"Not that piece of shit! Benny. Benicio Del Toro?"

"From the Bond movie?"

"No!"

"I'm confused."

"From fuckin Usual Suspects an uh uh"

"Swimming With Sharks"

"Oh my god, shut the fuck up"

"Wha-?"

"Shut up shut up shut up. Shut the fuck- If you

don't shut your fucking mouth and-... Ugh"

"Why are you so- OWWW! Cut that shit out. Totally uncalled for!"

"I said it. I said shut the fuck up. Did I not say shut the fuck-"

"Living Daylights"

"-up? No. See? Shut the fuck up. You have no idea what"

"No, you're right, uh View to a- No - Lisence to Kill"

"-you're talking- Yeah, I know, but what I'm saying is-"

"But he was in that one."

"-you don't. When someone says uh uh Jack Nicholson say uh uh-"

"Man Trouble"

"-exactly. You don't say- no you say uh uh-"

"Chinatown"

"Yeah"

"The Shining"

"Exactly"

"Batman"

"Are you shitting me? Batman?"

"What's the matter with Batman?"

"It's just"

"You don't like Batman?"

"No, I just-"

"You don't?"

"No-"

"Wait. You do or you do not like Batman?"

"I like- What I'm trying to say is I say Benicio Del Toro and immediately you think 'from the Bond movie'?"

"Excess Baggage"

"Homo."

"Queer."

"So, the show, right? Nolte and Benicio and you know like maybe Brando"

"Dead"

"I know he's fucking dead, it's not a real show."

"It's an idea."

"Yes, an idea for a show."

"Brando's dead."

"I know he's fucking dead. It doesn't matter."

"Missouri Breaks."

"Asshole, let me- It would be kinda like The View"

"With Rosie and shit?"

"I just mean the format, not the feel, obviously."

"'Cause I don't think Nolte would do-"

"I know he wouldn't. It's an idea for a sketch show."

"Comedy."

"No serious fucking drama, retard. Yes, comedy. It's an idea for-"

"The Upright Citizen's-"

"-a sketch for a- Oh for fuck's sake can you just say SNL or Monty Python-"

"-The State."

"-or something that your average fucking- Fine, yes Kids-"

"Say no more."

"-In the- Thank you. It's an idea"

"For like a sketch or the premise of a- OWWW! Don't!"

"OWWW! Son of a-"

"Why are you so violent? Seriously. What's wrong with you?"

"Just don't interrupt me. I don't want to hurt you."

"Then why'd you-"

"Because you won't let me get a simple fucking

thought across without-"

"Sorry."

"Thank you."

"Go on."

"Thank you. It's just an idea for a...

"What?"

"Now it's all blown out of proportion, it wont seem funny."

"Sure it will."

"No, now I've built it up and when you hear it you're gonna think 'Why the hell did he get so worked up over that?'"

"No c'mon. Now I gotta know."

"Fine, but it's not that funny."

"Okay, just tell me."

"Okay. It's just an idea for like a sketch on a, you know, sketch show that would be-"

"Like a recurring sketch?"

"Yeah maybe, but it would be like The View, you know a bunch of people sitting around talking about current events and shit."

"Wait. This is the show or the sketch?"

"The sketch."

"So, what's the show called?"

"Doesn't matter."

"'Course it does."

"I mean it doesn't matter what the name of the show is for the pur-"

"I think the name of a show is integral to-"

"-pose of appreciating the-"

"-the experience of that particular type of enter-"

"-idea of the sketch. Oh my god, shut- Integral?"

"-tainment. Yeah, integral. What of it, bitch?"

"Good usage."

"Thanks."

"Okay, so just pick your favorite sketch show and pretend, for the sake of all the souls in purgatory, that it's that one."

"In Living Color."

"Fine."

"Brando was still alive."

"Okay, yes"

"But Benicio Del Toro wasn't known then but okay okay okay come back. Yeah yeah yeah, I'm listening, okay it's a sketch about a show like The View..."

"Right. With like topics and shit."

"But instead of Rosie and Starr-"

"It's Nolte and Benicio, maybe Brando and like uh Bob Dylan and um Shane McGowan." "Who?"

"Nevermind. Uh, Ozzy Osbourne."

"Okay... I don't get it."

"See? This is why I didn't..."

"No, just explain it."

"It's really not funny if it's gotta be explained."

"I just want to have a clear idea of this. I'm sure I'll laugh. It sounds funny, I just want to-"

"Okay. Nolte, Del Toro, Dylan, Ozzy? They're sitting around talking about uh uh uh current events or celebrity gossip or some shit and-"

"Nobody can understand-"

"Exactly."

"That's hilarious!"

"You thinks so?"

"Shit yeah, man. Nolte's all 'Aarrarragh rrarrarragh rarrarragh' and then Dylan says 'Neeyah nee nay weeer' or something."

"Yeah, and I figure each week they could-"

"So it would be a recurring sketch?"

"Yeah, I guess so."

"Cool."

"Each week they could have another guest."

"Like The View."

"Exactly. And they could be like-"

"Totally lost and not able to understand, looking around like 'I'm gonna totally murder my agent'."

"Yeah, maybe, or think of this. Could be guests like uh uh"

"Politicians?"

"Maybe, but-"

"The real guys, maybe-"

"No. Shut up. Could be guests like uh maybe"

"A Klingon."

"Kling-?"

"On. From Star Trek."

"I know where they're-"

"Speaking, you know Klingon."

"Fine, yes have a Klingon on some time, but I"m thinking have on guests like Tom Waits or-"

"Some rapper."

"Huh?"

"You can understand them?"

"Nevermind. You get the idea."

"David Lynch."

"Stephen Hawking."

"Holy shit, now that's funny."

"Diane Rehm."

"Now you're just getting cruel."

"Funny though."

About the Author

Jedidiah Ayres' fiction has appeared in several books, magazines and online journals, he is the co-editor of the fiction anthologies Noir at the Bar and D*CKED. He is also the screenwriter of Mosquito Kingdom. He keeps the blog Hardboiled Wonderland.

Snubnose Press
Compact. Powerful. Classic.

SHORT STORY COLLECTIONS
The Chaos We Know - Keith Rawson
Monkey Justice - Patti Abbott
Gumbo Ya-Ya - Les Edgerton
Cold Rifts - Sandra Seamans
Old School - Dan O'Shea
A Bouquet of Bullets - Eric Beetner
The First Cut - John Kenyon
Bar Scars - Nik Korpon
Herniated Roots - Richard Thomas

NOVELS
Harvest Of Ruins - Sandra Ruttan
Hill Country - R. Thomas Brown
The Duplicate - Helen Fitzgerald
Old Ghosts - Nik Korpon
Nothing Matters - Steve Finbow
City Of Heretics - Heath Lowrance
Blood on Blood - Jim Wilsky & Frank Zafiro
Dig Two Graves - Eric Beetner
Ghost Money - Andrew Nette
Karma Backlash - Chad Rohrbacher

AND MANY MORE COMING SOON

Made in the USA
Middletown, DE
01 March 2015